THE COLD BROOK JOB

AN ENDLESS FRONTIER FOLKTALE

Brett Lurie

CONTENTS

Timeline of the Endless Frontier
All Titles Available Now!

04/19, 3766 *Sky Guard*

05/15, 3788 *The Rider in Black*

14/14, 3790 *The Case of the Gill Ripper*

07/22, 3799 *The Cold Brook Job*

09/17, 3799 *Of Duels and Debts*

11/01, 3800 *The Hunter and the Knight*

Cover Artwork and Design by Mushfiq A.K.

Interior Illustrations by Violet Bast

Edited by Tammy Salyer - Inspired Ink Editing

1st edition 2024

ISBN: 979-8-9897742-7-2(Paperback)

ISBN: 979-8-9897742-6-5 (e-Book)

Acknowledgements

To those who have found comfort and belonging in this world,
I invite you to join in another epic adventure of electric swords
and ancient sorcery. You have been wonderful companions
as we navigate the strange, uncharted territory of Eramaa. I
promise you, we have only taken our first steps. Thank you for
helping to blaze this trail.

ICE WYRM ISLE
DISCIPLE'S RAPTURE
SIREN SONG ISLE
WATCHER'S SHORE
HELIOS SUMMIT
MOUNT MORVIUS
SANCTUARY
RAVEN FORT
THE HOLY HARBOR
SILVERKEEP
LAKE SHAL
PEAKS OF PURIFICATION
ANDEO COAST

THE HIGH IMPERIUM

SH VALLEY

EEL'S MOUTH

HOLLOW MESA

COLD BROOK

DEN CREEK

ONYX CANYON

STGATE HARBOR

READBANK

TAL FLATS
VAELIZ ESTATE

CACTUSTOWN

ULTURE

THE VALLEY OF TOMBS

NTOM MESA

DRAELEKAR

I

THE BLACK ROAD

"'Paved with shadow, paved with ashes, paved with brimstone, the black road is all I know. I follow it by day, I follow it by night, its crooked lanes follow dark delights. Decry such carnal desires and never will you see these splintered paths of ecstasy. The call of the wild is breathless, without end. And in darkness my spirit will mend. Paved with shadow, paved with ashes, paved with brimstone, the black road is all I know.'"

The saloon's floorboards creaked with the steps of surrounding patrons, their passing chatter eerily quiet. Two men and one woman sat across from Breylu Dast, each with a common blue-grey shade of Vandeni skin.

"That's pretty good." The woman's head tilted as cigarillo smoke filtered through her gills. She folded her hands over the table. "One of yours?"

"No." Breylu Dast's glowing green eyes narrowed behind his circular spectacles. His voice crackled as he let out a chuckle. "Dralios Maelis, an old Imperial poet. I've always been fond of his rhythm and verse."

A faint scent of sizzling meats seeped from the kitchen. Clanking glasses rang from behind the bar. "So, what do you think?" asked one of the men across from Dast. He leaned on his forearms, trying to hide his shaking leg. "Do you think you'd like to meet our employer?"

"I very much would." Breylu leaned forward, brushing his poncho off his right shoulder. "You tell me he's just outside of town?"

"That's right."

"And I have to come alone?"

The woman nodded.

"Understood." Breylu's arm moved to his belt at a speed far from natural, with a faint buzzing sound. He drew his pistol and fired upon the three patrons who had joined him at his table. Before their faces could fully turn from nervous apprehension to shock, weaponized lightning bolts struck them in sequence, and they fell to the ground. Glasses shattered on the floor. Waiters, escorts and customers of the establishment backed away or ducked in panic. Breylu's head tilted as he stared at the bodies, still smoking and twitching.

Behind him, three more shock-cannon bolts rained from above. Breylu did not need to turn around to know that the shots came from Vinai of Oglund, his trusted sniper, taking care of any accomplices of the three who had shared Breylu's table or concerned onlookers who decided to play hero. Breylu holstered his weapon and smiled behind his snakeskin mask as the shots continued to rain down.

"Hello, Marshal's Department, there's been a—" The man two tables away was silenced with a gurgle. Nellik of Grathank held up the elderly Vandeni man by the throat, his forked reptilian tongue slithering as he pulled the man's face closer.

"Nellik," Breylu said with a calm authority. "Put him down."

"Sure thing, boss." Nellik slammed him against the ground, leaving him lying still. The Draekalagon hissed as he smashed the data system from which the old man was sending his transmission.

"Forgive the ruckus, Loney." Breylu gave the bartender a limp wave.

"Dast," the overweight, bald bartender said as he wiped his brow with a wet cloth. "You're supposed to warn me when something like this is about to happen!" He attempted to calm his patrons, assuring them that all was okay.

"Wasn't sure how this would unfold myself." Breylu adjusted his tall hat.

Loney's head shook as he beheld the broken glasses, shattered whisky bottles and flipped-over tables. "Look at this mess."

Stepping away, Breylu waved him off. "Put it on my tab."

Loney's round form deflated as he shook his head.

Nellik stepped to Breylu's side and crossed his arms, mirroring his superior's gesture. "Lawmen?"

Breylu's bright green eyes shifted to a deep purple. "Bounty hunters."

"Damn it."

Breylu looked to the tall draconic man with a tilt of his head.

"I owe Lynara three-hundred platinum."

Breylu turned away. "And how much do you owe me?"

"Who's counting?"

"I am."

A barrage of shock-cannon fire thundered from the streets. Nellik, Vinai and Breylu aimed their weapons toward the entrance of the saloon. Through the swinging doors tumbled not an adversary, but a man in a brown trench coat and a burgundy hat named Jarrus Thane. He aimed both pistols forward, smoke rising from the barrels.

Still in a kneeling position, he turned around and offered Breylu a crooked smile. "Sorry I'm late to the party, boss. Lynara was supposed to back me up, but she apparently had more important things to deal with."

"Who were you shooting at?" asked Nellik.

"I would assume *their* backup." Jarrus eyed the three bounty hunters Breylu had shot, lying on the floor. "They were running in here, shock-cannons drawn." He came to his feet and gave a shrug. "But they had to get by me, and..." He became distracted by a tall Vandeni woman in a shimmering sapphire-blue dress. "My trigger finger ain't so forgiving," he uttered, looking her up and down.

Nellik buried his face in his hand, wrapping his claws around his forehead.

"Pick one of them up on our way out," said Breylu. "We are going to need to question them."

"Oh, umm." Jarrus examined the lethality toggle on each of his pistols. "Yeah, that's gunna be an issue. They're all dead."

"Not a problem." Breylu picked out an undistinguished Vandeni man in the crowd, wearing a black coat that was slightly too small for him. "Giavi."

The man sprang out of his chair and stood tall before Dast, as if standing at attention. "Yes, boss."

"I'm still getting a slight pulse on that one." He pointed toward the female bounty hunter he had shot. "Think you can keep her blood pumping for a few more hours?"

Giavi leaned down and placed a pair of spectacles over his eyes before putting on his gloves and feeling her pulse. "With a shot of adrenaline and a few nervous system stims..." He tapped a few buttons on his goggles, which buzzed and beeped in turn. "Shouldn't be a problem."

"Good." Breylu nodded. "Let's get out of here." After tossing Loney a large platinum coin, Breylu stepped toward the exit, with Nellik trailing.

"Umm, isn't someone gunna help me carry her?" Giavi asked.

"You can handle it," replied Nellik. "She ain't that big."

"She's bigger than me!"

"Build some muscle, Giavi."

As he walked, Breylu put out a transmission. "Crow, have we picked up any curious badges?"

"Yes, sir," a smoky female voice said through the communications implant in his ear. "But I patched into their network. They think you're in one of the saloons on the other side of town."

"A clever diversion," said Vinai via transmission, who still watched like a hawk from the saloon's upper level.

"Yes, the diversion is ready," said a different female voice with a strange, eager rhythm.

"Lynara," Breylu said with a harsh grunt. "Where have you been?"

"Here, there, everywhere. Hard on the job. Always prepared. Always ready."

"You were supposed to be backing up Jarrus. Get ready to get out of..." Breylu stopped his instruction as he pondered his demolition expert's words. "What diversion?"

Lynara did not respond. Breylu pushed his way through the swinging doors and rushed outside. He scanned the street. The electric glow of the power transfer cylinders over the sidewalks and the blue streetlamps showed no immediate threat. Riders passed at the intersection down the road. Concerned onlookers looked out the windows from tall metal buildings. It was only a matter of time before the lawmen would find them.

"Everyone," shouted Breylu. "Saddle up. It's time to—"

As he spoke, the intersection ignited in a flash. Breylu's glowing green eyes shifted to a deep blue as the white light vanished, leaving behind a dancing orange flame.

Jarrus rushed out of the saloon with pistols drawn and covered his eyes as he looked down the street. "What the hell happened?"

Lynara's maniacal laughter surged through the communication devices of the gang.

Jarrus nodded and let out a sigh. "I'd say it's time we got the hell out of here."

"Indeed." Breylu ran down the sidewalk's stairs and over to the trough outside the saloon. He climbed atop his trugan's saddle and locked his boots in its stirrups. The beast was long and slender, with scales of such a deep shade of maroon that they appeared black under the dark skies. But her golden-red eyes pierced through the veil of dusk. "Run, Maedreth. Run as a windstorm on the plains." With those words, and a kick from her rider, Maedreth took off down the street. Pedestrians and other trugan riders cleared the way for her sprint.

The other Shadow Riders from the saloon followed. Breylu choked up on Maedreth's reins, slowing her pace. The other trugan did not have as many cybernetic speed enhancements, and Breylu had no intention of leaving his gang behind.

He looked back. Athenis, the world's orbital star, left its final declining rays of blue light on the city they were escaping from. "Lynara, Crow, where are you?" he asked via transmission as the wind roared by.

"We're moving out through the city's southern exit," replied Crow. "We'll meet you at the rendezvous point."

"Copy that. And, Lynara," he growled, "you and I are going to have a little conversation."

"I'll check my schedule." Lynara hummed a tune to herself before replying. "Yep, no problem. I can fit you in, boss."

"Is that so?"

"Yep!"

Breylu groaned and rolled his eyes. He was about to ask Gi-avi the condition of the prisoner when his cybernetic sensory augments warned him of danger. While not consciously aware of what this danger could be, his instincts told him to bring his trugan to a sudden stop. A few meters ahead of him, right along his previous riding trajectory, a bolt of lightning raced across the grassy plains and struck the ground.

"Vinai!" yelled Breylu. "Sniper out there. Trace the shot."

Vinai was already looking through the scope in the general direction of where the cannon fire had come from.

Giavi, now quite a distance ahead, began to slow down, eyes on the horizon.

"No!" Breylu yelled. "Giavi, don't slow down!"

He slapped the reins upon Maedreth's neck. The trugan responded by sprinting with all her might toward Giavi and his trugan. Breylu's reflex enhancements again warned of danger. Maedreth dashed with all her might toward the medic. As she crossed before him, another sniper shot thundered from the distance.

The blast of lightning, intended for Giavi, instead struck Maedreth. The electricity coursed throughout her body and up Breylu's cybernetic leg. The beast collapsed, sending Breylu propelling forward and skidding across the blue-grey grass.

With a groan, he lifted his head. Vinai slowed her trugan and fired two shots into the woods to the west. She rested her rifle over her shoulder. "Scratch two," she said with a hiss through the communication system. She and the other members of the gang turned to check on Breylu.

He stood up, patting down his slacks and poncho. The gashes on his skin did not reveal blood but rather cybernetic musculature made from a soft metal alloy. His mechanical leg whined with his step, forcing him to walk with a slight limp.

"You alright, boss?" asked Nellik as he brought his trugan to a stop before him.

"I'm alright."

Nellik thrust his fist at Giavi. "You idiot. Why did you slow down?"

"I'm sorry," replied the combat medic with a deflated sigh. "I panicked when the boss said there was a sniper."

Breylu shook his head and waved him off. "It's alright, Giavi."

A reptilian groan forced Breylu to turn around. On the ground Maedreth lay, smoke rising from her scales and legs bent outward in an unnatural position. She tried to stand but could not make it more than a few inches off the ground.

Her vertical eye slits widened as they found her rider. She grunted and whimpered as he knelt on one knee to offer his hand. Her eyes shut as he ran his finger from her horn to her nose. "Long have you borne me as a burden," he said with a rasp in his staticky voice. "Long have you stood at my side as a fierce ally. Long have you been a guide to this gang." He held back a whimper. "Long have you been my friend."

Maedreth writhed in pain and unleashed a guttural growl. Breylu drew his pistol and made sure that the lethality toggle was turned all the way up. "May your light find the stars. One day, I shall find you there, and we shall ride again."

Breylu discharged his weapon into Maedreth's head. Her jaw expanded for a moment, before her eyes rolled back. After she jolted back and forth with the electric currents for several seconds, the electricity subsided and her body stilled.

Jarrus and Nellik took off their hats. Giavi began to sniffle. Vinai said a prayer.

"Come on," said Breylu. "Let's get out of here before more show up." He stepped beside Jarrus and his green trugan. "Mind if I ride with you?"

"Sure thing, boss," said Jarrus.

Vinai looked through her scope toward the forest where she had shot the two bounty hunters who had fired upon the gang. "I incapped them in case you wanted to take them in for questioning, Breylu. Do you?"

Breylu cast a final glance at Maedreth's body before climbing atop Jarrus' saddle. "No."

Vinai fired two shots into the woods, and the gang rode into the night, through the vast plains of Vanda.

II
FRIENDS AND FOES

"You don't mind, do you?" Crow asked, pointing to the thin white cigarillo in her mouth.

"Not at all," replied Breylu, resting back in the mechanical operating chair, his cybernetic leg detached from his body. "I can turn off my sensory perceptions, Crow."

"Of course."

Crow lit her cigarillo and leaned over the leader of the gang. His long torso expanded with his breath. The musculature around his abdomen contracted, unnaturally defined for how thin of a man he was. He tensed as Crow ran her soldering iron across the exposed cybernetic musculature on his chest, but his expression remained neutral.

Bright blue lights on the cylindrical ceiling shined on the outlaw's bare chest. Crow admired the perfect definition of black musculature, crafted from a soft metal alloy. Hydraulic gears beneath his skin turned when Breylu moved his neck or rotated his arm. His metal joints snapped in place when he adjusted his positioning.

He was fascinating. And Crow had the privilege of seeing how each circuit, each prosthetic, each digital processing core functioned in cohesion to sustain this man. If one could still call him a man.

"Did I ever tell you about the time that Nellik, Jarrus and I took on the entire Black Wall Gang by ourselves?" His voice crackled with excitement, but his glowing green eyes stared blankly at the ceiling.

"Don't think so, sir." She flipped a switch on her soldering iron, converting the device to a welder. Sparks reflected on her visor as she ran the tool across his chest, sealing the exposed wires behind metalized marrow. Her smile released a waft of cigarillo smoke.

"We were surrounded by those rotten low-lives in the middle of the street. All the townsfolk in Rust Road watched from their windows as we took cover behind some supply crates outside the local saloon. They were closing in, trying to flush us from hiding. Then Nellik, the crazy bastard, climbs to the top of the saloon and starts hurling grenades at the Black Wall scum. Jarrus and I look to each other and come out cannons blazing. Next thing we know, they're all dead."

Crow chuckled. "A few dozen small-town bandits against the three deadliest men in Vanda? They never stood a chance."

Breylu's voice shook with a chuckle. "The best part is that the mayor of Rust Road paid us twelve thousand platinum. I don't think he knew who we were."

Crow laughed along as she sat up straight and turned her head, focusing on the exposed cybernetic musculature and metal bone that she had spent hours repairing. "You're in good shape on your muscle and bone damage. I replaced some of the older tissue that looked like it was nearing expiration while I was in there."

"Very good."

"You're going to want to see Giavi about skin grafting to cover your wounds. Not my area of expertise."

"That can wait."

"Now, let me see if that leg is ready." Crow turned to her workbench.

She grabbed a rag and wiped a streak of oil from her grey skin. On a base atop the table sat a black cybernetic leg. Crow tapped an icon on her optical visor, and the device shifted to a blue tint.

"Okay," she said with a drag of her cigarillo. "It's ready to go, sir." She picked up the leg and cleared her throat. "Since you have it off, I thought that I should share with you a development that I have made."

She reached into the workbench drawer and pulled out a hexagonal device that fit in the palm of her hand. Lights flashed on the corners when she flipped a switch on the side. "I built an upgrade for your leg. It should help with movement and flexibility. But—"

"Put it in," Breylu ordered.

"But I should warn you, it will sever some of the natural neural connections to your—"

"Put in in," he repeated.

"Understood. It will just be a moment." A grin found its way to Crow's grey lips as she attached the device just below the knee of his cybernetic leg. It clicked in place, a perfect fit.

She turned around and stepped toward the leader of the Moon Shadow Riders, his leg in her hands. "Ready?"

"Yes."

She lined up the leg with his thigh and began to drill it into place. His body twitched with the hum of the power tool and the grinding metal of screws locking in. Again, Breylu Dast's face showed no sign of pain.

"Did I tell you about when I beat Kasta Krane to the Totem of Akliar? And she ran like a coward?"

Crow forced a smile. "No, sir."

"I told her if she came out to face me one-on-one, the totem would be hers, and my gang would let her walk free. But she ran into the shadows. Like she always does." He winced. For the first time since Crow had begun work, he *did* look to be in pain. "Any sign of her?"

She knew that question was coming. "No, sir. Nothing." A sigh slipped between her words.

His ghostly gaze loomed above. "Am I boring you?"

"Not at all." Her pale-blue eyes sparkled in the reflection of the lights. "I don't have any updates for you. I wish I did. But Krane knows you are after her. She does not have a permanent address, nor does she seem to stay in one place for very long."

"She still doing work for that pirate?"

"Last I heard, yes."

"Keep an eye on that."

"Of course."

Breylu's voice fell low and dissonant. "Still no luck hacking into her private network? Her communications? Her digital records?"

"No." She lifted his knee for better access to the underside of his leg. "Whatever encryption code she is using is quite effective. She doesn't leave any footprints on the satellite network."

"Keep looking."

"If I ever can take a shot at her, I will. I'm sure you would pay a good bonus for her head."

Aside from the droning of the drill, the room fell silent. Crow stole a glance at her employer to find him staring down on her like a hungry shark. His glowing green eyes burned with such rage that his pupils threatened to burst through his cybernetic corneas.

Crow stopped drilling. "Sorry, I—"

"Crow..." Breylu's voice shook as he spoke her name, drawing out the sound until it faded to cold static. "You are to track her, hunt her, lead me to her. But Kasta Krane... she is mine."

"Yes." She cleared her throat before she could stop herself from asking, "Why do you hate her so much?"

Those glowing eyes narrowed. His head tilted. "Why do you think?"

"I'm sorry, sir. That was a foolish question." She returned her focus to reattaching his mechanical leg.

But he reached down and stuck a finger under her chin. With unnatural strength, he lifted her face to force eye contact. "Why do you think?" he asked again, venom seeping into his words.

"You've told me the story, sir. I know how personal it is."

"Is that what you think?" His back rose from the chair. He leaned over Crow like a coiled cobra ready to strike. "I do not hate Kasta Krane for the evil she has brought on me. I hate Kasta Krane for the evil she has brought on the world. She must be opposed. Kasta Krane is a bloodthirsty demon who wears a mask of mercy.

"'When a demon leaves a mark upon the living soul, a hate shall spread like sickness that no tonic can control. A mask of virtue it shall wear and it will walk alone. Until this evil is expelled, its torment shall be known.'"

"I like that one," said Crow, his finger still under her chin. "Maelis?"

"No," he said, his tone suddenly light. "Ara Rith."

"That was my second guess."

"Of course it was." Breylu released his grip on her chin and leaned back in the chair.

Crow let out a quiet sigh of relief. "We're almost done." She put the drill down and reached for her pocket-sized utility tool. "I just need to recalibrate a few of the connections." She rerouted power from the leg to the new device. After she connected the conduits, a steady hum of wireless electricity flowed from the mechanical leg to the device and back to the leg in an alternating current. "Alright. Go on, test it out."

Breylu stood up and took an awkward step. After stumbling over his own feet a few times, he found his footing and discovered a more natural stride. He lifted his leg, bending his knee back and forth. "I..." The typical authority in his voice faded away. "I haven't felt this much control in my leg since"—his staticky voice shook as he looked to Crow—"in a long time."

"Does it feel okay? I can adjust it if you would like."

"No." He stepped toward her and placed a hand on her shoulder. "It's perfect. Thank you."

"My pleasure, sir."

"You keep calling me sir," he said with an amused tone.

"Old habit," Crow said with a grin as she put out her cigarillo on the floor. "I can stop if it bothers you."

"Not in the slightest."

He laid a finger on his ear and answered an incoming transmission. "Nellik," he said, cold neutrality returning to his voice. "Talk to me." He paused and listened before stating, "We'll be right in." He tapped his ear again, disconnecting the transmission.

"What's the word?" asked Crow.

"She's awake." He put on his dark red dress shirt and reattached his specs, his eyes bringing their circular shape to a piercing glow. "Care to join me?"

Crow stood up and placed her tall black hat on her head. "It would be an honor."

After stepping through the dim red lighting of the Moon Shadow Riders' stronghold, Breylu Dast came to a tall steel door. He punched in a code on the digital panel and the door opened. Nellik, Jarrus and Vinai stood around a medical bed, where the surviving female bounty hunter lay with an IV connected to her arm. The tubes led to a heart monitor, where Giavi tapped on the screen, examining his patient's vitals.

"How's she looking?" asked Breylu, crossing his arms.

The bounty hunter, chained to the bed, backed up, with panic pasted to her blue-grey face. "Please, please. Don't hurt—"

"I'm not talking to you," Breylu interrupted with a dismissive wave. "Giavi, damage report."

"She's doing fine," the blue-skinned medic said, looking over his shoulder, past his half turned-up collar. "She's got a little nervous system and brain damage. But nothing too problematic for your purposes."

The bounty hunter's jaw dropped. "Br-brain damage?"

Breylu held out a finger. "I am *not* talking to you." He turned around and faced Lynara, who was leaning against the wall, hiding her eyes with the brim of her hat. "You," he said with bitterness in his voice. "What were you thinking?" He stepped toward her and trapped her against the wall with his imposing frame.

"I know, boss. I messed up." She looked up, scratching her chin. "Napalm was a poor choice. Should have used nitro."

"I didn't ask you for any detonations," he said with a shake of his head. "You have to listen to me."

"I agree," Lynara said, raising a finger. "Voltage traps next time. Very effective. Little collateral. Still makes a statement."

"Lynara, unless I call for you, you need to remain on standby. You were supposed to back up Jarrus."

The woman shrugged, blowing her frizzy black hair out of her face. "I did!"

Crow could sense Breylu's rising anger. "Lynara!" she said with a harsh whisper. When the demolitions expert looked her way, Crow shook her head and raised her eyebrows.

"Sorry, boss." Lynara's eyes darted back to Breylu, uneasiness in her voice. "I'll... I'll do better next time."

"Good," Breylu said, turning around.

"I'll make sure to set off the bombs closer to the marshal's department. That'll really throw them off."

"Why you little..."

Crow jumped between her employer and the gangly Vandeni woman. "I think what Lynara *meant* to say is that she will wait for your permission before setting off any explosions in a populated town." She flashed Lynara a sharp glare. "*Right?*"

Lynara paused in confusion for a moment before finally saying, "Right," in an uneasy, strained voice.

Breylu shook his head and looked to the prisoner in the medical bed. "Who sent you?"

Her lip trembled as she tried to back away, but she was already against the head of the bed.

"Yes, I am talking to you now." Breylu's boots thumped against the stone floor as he approached the bounty hunter. "Who are you working for?"

"Ash Valley Marshal's Department." She swallowed. "They—they sent us to bring you in when you came into town."

Breylu began to chuckle. That chuckle turned into roaring laughter. Nellik joined, followed by Jarrus. Eventually Giavi did as well. Lynara and Vinai remained silent. Crow smiled but was focused on her data system.

"So, here is how this is going to work." He rested his cybernetic leg at the foot of the bed. "I'm going to ask you some questions. Some of them, I already know the answer to."

"Then what's the point of asking?" asked Nellik.

"Glad you asked." His green eyes shifted to blue, then purple. "I want to know how honest she is." He spoke of the bounty hunter in the third person, though he never looked away from her. "Her level of honesty is directly tied to her chance of survival."

The prisoner breathed rapidly before averting her gaze and letting out an uneasy sigh. "What would you like to know?"

"Your name?"

"Geldra Marlsson."

"Where are you from?"

"I was born in Dreadbank. I live just outside Vulture now."

Breylu turned to Crow, who looked to her data system. Her screen was filled with old records. She gave him a subtle nod.

"Why'd you become a bounty hunter?"

"Umm—to make money." She shrugged and eyed the outlaws around the room. "Why does anyone?"

"I don't know," answered Breylu. "But why did you?"

"Excitement, I guess."

Those glowing green eyes of Breylu Dast filled with disappointment.

"I wanted to be a law official," she said with a sigh. "But I never made it past cadet."

Crow consulted her data system and nodded to Breylu again.

A muffled chuckle seeped from behind his snakeskin mask. "A noble pursuit, indeed." His voice darkened in an instant as he asked, "Who are you working for?"

She shook her head. "I can't say. He'll kill me."

"What a coincidence. Your employer and I have something in common." Breylu pointed to the Vandeni man behind him. "Jarrus, kill her."

Jarrus drew his pistols and took aim.

"Wait, wait, wait, wait, wait!" she raised her hands. The beeping of the heartrate monitor accelerated. Giavi turned around to check on her vitals once more. "Will you let me live if I talk?"

Breylu shrugged. "Can't hurt your chances."

"Fraedrik Gor." She shut her eyes and hid her face. "We were hired by Fraedrik Gor."

"That scum," Breylu said with a groan. "We had a ceasefire."

"Not anymore." Her dark brown eyes stole a glance at Breylu. "He hired us to take you out for that smuggling op you have going in East Gate Harbor."

"Since when is that his territory?"

She raised her hands. "Listen, I'm a cannon for hire. I don't know all the politics. He thinks you are getting too big. He wanted to send a message to the other gangs that he is still the top cannon in central Vanda."

"Is he?" Breylu chuckled and looked to his pistoleer. "What do you think, Jarrus?"

Jarrus twirled his pistols around the tips of his fingers, causing the prisoner to flinch and cower. "I don't think that fat cat could even fit his finger around a trigger, boss."

Nellik smacked him on the back, and the pair shared a laugh.

Breylu's eyes narrowed on his captive, his head tilting to the side. "How much did he offer you?"

"Ten thousand platinum for you. One thousand each for the rest of the gang."

"That's it?" Jarrus shook his head. "That's small-town wanted-poster money." He tilted the brim of his hat up with the barrel of his pistol. "I say we go on down to Indigo Cove and show him what we're made of."

Vinai tapped her clawed foot on the floor. "Certainly explains the lack of quality on this team of bounty hunters that attacked us."

"Indeed," Breylu said. "Gor has always preferred quantity over quality in his organization. One of the reasons that he and I never worked well together."

"One of many," Nellik added.

The room remained silent save for the beeping triplets of the heart monitor and the low hum of the power transfer cylinders supplying electricity to the lights and the life support system.

"What else do you know?" Breylu finally asked.

"N-nothing, there's nothing else," the prisoner uttered with a gasp, as if she were out of breath.

"Alright then. Jarrus, make it quick."

Jarrus aimed his pistols at the woman in the hospital bed. Giavi raised his hands as if he were going to stand between the shooter and his patient. But he did not rush to her defense. He backed away.

Crow looked to her data system, scanning for any information she could find on this Fraedrik Gor. She knew Breylu would want a full report on his current activities and whereabouts after their prisoner was disposed of. She had to prepare notes for a briefing.

"Wait, wait, wait!" Geldra screamed. "You said you'd let me live if I was honest."

"I said it couldn't hurt your chances," Breylu replied with a sinister tone. "And it didn't. But you, Geldra, are what we call a liability. I don't believe in liabilities." He turned to his pistoleer. "Jarrus, as you were."

"I can tell you something else!" She thrashed within the chains, but they only further constricted her torso as she struggled. "I know what Gor's next move is."

Breylu raised his finger toward Jarrus, and the triggerman brought his pistol to an at-ease position. "Oh, do you?" asked the gang's leader. "I thought you did not know anything else, that you didn't follow any of the... politics."

"I don't. But he already hired my crew for the next job." She cleared her throat and looked down. "Please let me live if I tell you. Because he won't."

"Speak," ordered Breylu.

"Gor is moving two hundred thousand in freshly minted platinum."

The leader of the gang chuckled. "And why would he make one of his hired hands privy to such information?"

"Well, he—he didn't *tell* me," the woman stuttered. Her eyes darted around the room. "He hired me and my team to guard a caravan. I just kind of figured it out."

"You just kind of figured it out," Breylu reiterated with a scoff. "This is a waste of my time. Jarrus..."

"No! Please, don't!"

Crow quickly swiped through her data system, deciphering codes on the satellite network and reading transcripts from unencrypted digital conversations. "Where did you say the caravan was heading?"

The prisoner's eyes wheeled to Crow. "Umm—" Her breathing was rapid and uncontrolled.

Crow stepped in front of Jarrus so that the woman would not see his pistol. The tech expert spoke with a soft, calming tone. "The caravan is leaving from his manor on the outskirts of Indigo Cove. Where is he moving the stash?"

She swallowed before uttering, "Cold Brook."

"When?"

"The shipment is set to depart in three days."

With a slight grin, Crow handed her data system to Breylu. "She's not lying."

Breylu's glowing eyes darkened as he read aloud. "'NOTICE: Citizens of Cold Brook. Main Street will be closed on 08/02/3799. Please plan accordingly.'"

"I don't buy any of this," hissed Nellik. "It's either a coincidence or *she* is finally going to make her move to stab us in the back." His clawed finger extended toward Crow, then to the woman in bed. "These two she-devils are probably cohorts. They're setting us up."

Crow gave the Draekalagon a smile and a nod. "I wouldn't dream of it. You're all far too kind to me."

Nellik hissed at her, leaving Crow feeling both disgraced and flattered, but mostly flattered. Her smile persevered.

Breylu crossed his arms and looked down on his captive. "What else do you know?"

"Umm." She swallowed, hiding her eyes. "There are ten, no… twelve carts. One or two will carry the platinum."

"And the rest?"

Her eyes crawled up at him. "The brass. Bounty hunters, triggermen, assassins. Every gang and merc crew that he's ever flipped a coin to is on this job."

"Lots of enemies in one place," Jarrus said with a crooked grin. "Target practice, anyone?"

"I'll light 'em up and send 'em running," Lynara said with hunger in her eyes. "Running right to your crosshairs."

The pistoleer twirled his weapons and turned to her. "A day on the job, Lynara. Day on the job."

"Anything else?" Breylu's abrupt interjection silenced the rest of his gang.

Geldra shook her head. "That's all I know. I swear. That's really it."

"Why have you shared this with me?"

She looked up at him, confused.

"Why did you help us?"

"Because..." She closed her eyes, choosing her next words carefully. "Because I don't want to die."

"You really don't want to die?"

With tears forming in her brown eyes, she managed a single shake of her head.

"Crow?" Breylu turned his head toward her.

"Yes, sir?" She stepped forward and stood at attention, a habit she had been meaning to break.

"Have you finished that spinal monitoring device that you told me about?"

"Umm." Crow cleared her throat. "I have the prototype ready, yes."

"Good. Please bring it to me."

"Sir, if I may. The device still needs refinement for—"

"I said go get it." With a groaning deep breath, he added, "Please."

"Yes, sir."

Crow left the room and walked down the hallway toward her workstation. 'I have no desire to see her dead,' she thought. 'But I don't know that this is any better.'

When Crow returned to the recovery room, she held a cylindrical chrome device between her index finger and thumb. Jarrus leaned over the captive bounty hunter, bragging about his unmatched record at the Cactustown shooting range.

Breylu turned to Crow and motioned to the bounty hunter. "Proceed."

"Giavi should do it," Crow was quick to reply.

"Very well."

Giavi looked to Crow, uneasy concern on his boyish blue face. "What is this?" His voice dropped to a whisper as Crow approached. "What's going on?"

She presented him with the device that glowed in blue and magenta.

"Oh come on, not that." Giavi looked to the floor and shook his head. "She's my patient, boss. I can't do that to her."

"Do you want your patient to live?" asked Breylu.

Giavi nodded.

"Then proceed, Giavi."

"What is it?" asked Geldra. "What's going on?" She fidgeted, constricted by her shackles.

Breylu placed a foot on her bed. "You have not lied to me. And you have provided me with information of the... utmost value." He chuckled. "You did not even lie to me about your reasons for providing me with this information." His voice crackled as it fell to a hushed whisper. "And for that... I thank you. You shall be rewarded with your life."

Giavi loaded the cylindrical device into a sterling-silver medical drill with a fine needle point at the end.

"What is that?" asked Geldra. "What are you doing?"

Giavi gave the drill a few test spins. The device droned with a whining hum. "Hold still," he instructed.

As he brought the surgical tool toward her neck, she did anything but hold still. She squirmed, struggled and screamed.

"Nellik, hold her down," ordered Giavi. "Please."

Nellik of Grathank rushed to the bed and pinned the woman down, his hands on her shoulders. "This will end very poorly for you if you struggle."

"There is one issue," Breylu continued, his hand flamboyantly following the rhythm of his words, as though he were conducting an orchestra. "You displayed a complete lack of loyalty in your confession to me. I do not trust those who are disloyal." His glowing eyes narrowed. "Though to give you the benefit of the doubt, your prior employer likely did not give you much... motivation for loyalty."

Giavi shoved the needle inside her neck. The device beeped as it spun within her flesh, then flashed green. With a hushed metallic sound, the cylindrical device dislodged from the drill and attached itself to the woman's neck. She whimpered and hyperventilated as Giavi pulled the drill from her body and placed a strip of gauze over the wound to contain the spray of blood.

Crow turned away and shut her eyes.

"Well, I am going to change that." Breylu raised a finger, as though he were just coming up with the idea he was about to share. "You have the opportunity to act as an affiliate of the Moon Shadow Riders. Use your contacts to aid in our business ventures, inform us of any of our rivals' actions throughout the continent, do our bidding when we deem you fit for a task. In return, you will receive our protection, our hospitality, our good graces... and *our* loyalty."

"You..." The captive woman's eyes glazed over as Giavi placed a bandage on her throat. "You want me to be a Moon Shadow Rider?"

"The only Moon Shadow Riders are those who are in this room." He shrugged and opened his arms. "But our affiliates reign over the continent, not a part of our gang, but a part of our operations. Free to pursue their own interests, so long as they do not conflict with ours.

"That device in your neck will inform us of your where-abouts and verbal communications. If you try to remove it or betray the trust that I have placed in you, Crow has installed a little fail-safe."

He motioned to Crow, who stepped forward. "One touch"—she pointed to her data system—"and the device will explode in your neck."

"Are we clear?" asked Breylu.

The bounty hunter nodded.

"Good." He turned around and made for the door. "Return to Gor. Tell him that you failed to kill me. But inform him that we are weak and no longer a threat, that we have fled into hiding." He pointed to Vinai. "Give her one of the older trugan."

"Wait, wait," Giavi said with a stutter. "She's not well enough to ride. I need to monitor her for at least another sixty hours."

"Yes, I agree," said Crow. "We need to make sure the device is stable and—"

"You told me the device was ready, Crow," Breylu uttered. "It *was* ready, was it not?"

Crow's breath froze as his beaming eyes left an imprint on her corneas. "Yes, sir."

"Good. Help Giavi get her ready." He turned around in the doorway and addressed the gang. "Briefing room. One hour."

III

THE SEAT OF POWER

As the bounty hunter limped through the halls of the stronghold, Giavi let out an uneasy sigh. *Another* patient would not see the full extent of his care. 'At least the boss let this one live,' he thought. Her balance faltered. Giavi wrapped his hands around her arms to guide her steps, though he struggled to keep her upright. "Take it easy for a moment," he said. "Deep breaths, lassie. In and out."

His patient did as instructed. Her lungs whistled and her body twitched.

"How do you feel?" asked Crow from behind. She took a scan with her optical visor, no doubt checking her vitals. "Any pain or stiffness in the injection sight?"

Geldra cuffed the back of her neck, rotating her head. "There's this... clicking noise whenever I turn my head. And a sharp pain at the top of my spine."

"Interesting," said Crow, typing notes on her data system. "And how severe is this pain?"

"Crow!" Giavi addressed her with moaning frustration. "Now is not the time."

Crow stood over Giavi, her shadow extended by the breadth of her black coat. "When do you propose the time is, Giavi?" Her tone was condescending and dismissive, as if she were talking to a child. "If I do not take notes on the subject now, I may never get the opportunity."

Giavi wanted to push back against Crow's crude comments, but he found himself unable to speak, frozen by her icy-blue eyes. "You're right," he uttered. "I'm sorry."

Geldra cleared her throat and asked, "When you say the subject, you mean me?"

Crow nodded.

"And when you say you may never get the opportunity…"

"My, my. Perceptive, aren't we?" Crow grabbed her by the arm and dragged her down the hallway. "Come on, let's get you on the road. Tell me, do you feel any lightheadedness or confusion?"

"Umm, I… I don't—uhh—"

"We'll go with yes on that one."

Giavi scampered behind, occasionally laying a hand on Geldra's back. Crow was so easily able to pull the captive bounty hunter along, like she was taking her house fox on a leisurely stroll. 'It's because she's got that Imperial stature,' Giavi thought as he observed the hacker's frame. 'Tall and broad with a natural strength that you'd never find in a Vandeni, much less a little Rogue lad like me.'

They stepped outside the stronghold. Twinkling stars danced across the sky. The last rays of Athenis breached the horizon to the west, and the moons rose in opposition in the golden dusk over seas of spiraling ridges. A violet-eyed owl observed from the top of the stable as they approached, offering a low hoot in welcome.

Crow leaned Geldra against one of the wooden posts. Vinai of Oglund stepped out of one of the stalls, dragging a trugan by the reins. The beast's eyes were droopy, almost sad. His yellow hide had turned pale, sagging on his face and under his chin.

"This is Tuslavar," said Vinai. "He doesn't have much for speed anymore. But he'll remain true to his rider so long as you show him respect. Treat him well, and he'll make sure you survive the desert. Without protest."

Giavi handed Geldra a hessian sack. "Be sure you take the pills in there once every four hours. There's also some nighthawk jerky and dried fruit with some nuts. It ain't much but it will get you through the night until you reach Platinum Hill. Be sure to ration your water."

"Speaking of platinum," Crow said, reaching into her coat and retrieving a handful of coins. "A down payment from Mister Dast," she said, stuffing the clinking currency into the rider's pocket. "Make sure you save enough for travel to Indigo Cove. Remember, you are *not* to go anywhere else. If Mister Dast comes even under the slightest suspicion that you have another agenda..." She pointed to her data system, which displayed a digital rendering of the device that Giavi had planted in the woman's neck. Crow's finger drifted to a red icon marked "DETONATE."

Geldra gasped but nodded in agreement.

"Good," said Crow.

Vinai unbound Geldra from her shackles and helped her to the top of the old trugan's back.

"Don't I get a shock-cannon?" the woman asked.

Vinai shook her head.

Crow reached into her coat pocket once more and pulled out a small device. "You will take this, though. Use it only to contact Mister Dast and myself. Contact anyone else—"

"Yeah," Geldra interrupted. She pointed to her neck. "I get it."

Giavi took an uncertain step forward. "You can use it to contact me as well if you are feeling any disorientation, chest pain, severe swings in mood or—"

"Giavi," Crow interrupted. "That'll be enough."

Giavi hid his eyes and nodded.

"You're a sweet kid." Geldra's head turned as she analyzed the medic. "How'd you end up with this band of ruffians?"

Giavi shrugged and looked to Crow and Vinai, then to Geldra. "They're my family."

"Some family," she uttered with disdain.

"Let's get you moving." Crow's order was direct, but gentle. "Ride south. The mapping system will not turn on until you're one hundred miles out. You'll never find this fortress again. Unless we want you to. And if you try..."

"I got it," the bounty hunter growled. "Your infected Imperial claws are in my neck. And you'll kill me if I talk." She spit in Crow's direction. "Scum of the north."

Crow approached Geldra. "Scum of the north," she repeated with bitterness on her tongue. Her grey skin shifted to blood-red. But Crow halted when she noticed Vinai's golden gaze following her from the shadows. "Look." She extended a hand and her voice softened. The natural grey of her skin began to return. "If you prove an asset to Mister Dast, I will take that device out of your neck. Prove your loyalty and earn your freedom."

"Earn my freedom," the Vandeni woman reiterated with a shake of her head. After a moment of silent reflection, Geldra directed her mount forward, and the old beast listened. "Thanks," she said with a glance toward Giavi. Then, her steed galloped into the horizon at an unnatural speed. Trails of dust spread in the wake of the yellow trugan's gallop, then dissipated.

Giavi let out a sigh of relief as his back slumped against the wall of the stable.

"Prepare for the meeting," said Vinai as she walked away.

"Understood," replied Crow

As Vinai left their presence, Crow looked to Giavi with a playful tilt of her head. "Family? You truly think of me as family, Giavi?"

With a nervous grin, Giavi turned to her. "Of course."

She wrapped her arm around his neck. "I am touched." They walked toward the building, Crow dragging him along. Giavi clasped an arm to her waist.

"The Shadow Riders are the greatest family I have ever known," said Giavi. "I'd lay me life down for each and every one of ye."

Crow gave a slight grin as they moved along. While she had only been an official member of the gang for two months, Giavi felt as though he had known her for years. Yet, he felt as though he never *could* know this woman of many shades. As they entered the doorway, Giavi wondered how a warm embrace could feel so cold.

The Moon Shadow Riders gathered around the table. Breylu sat at the head, with Nellik and Jarrus on either side. Vinai and Lynara sat across from one another in the middle seats, and Giavi sat across from Crow at the opposite end.

"Two hundred thousand platinum," said Breylu. Over twenty-eight point five for each of us. Everyone okay with the usual twenty percent set aside into business expense funds?"

"That's fine."

"Yes."

"Of course."

"Twenty-two thousand each."

"Wait!" Giavi groaned and clutched the table, looking away when the eyes of the rest of the gang swiveled to him. "We're not going to take a vote on whether or not we proceed with this operation?"

"Vote?" Breylu laughed and leaned forward. "Everyone seems in agreement that this is a worthwhile venture."

The rest of the gang nodded.

"Unless you have a dissenting opinion, Giavi?"

The combat medic's brain flooded with dozens of reasons *not* to rob this caravan. The lack of information they currently had on the convoy, and the mercenaries protecting it. The risk of death versus the reward of the payout was not worth it. Not to mention, the inevitable gang war that would ensue in the aftermath. Months and months of violence. The eyes of the other Shadow Riders focused on him with such piercing cynicism that he wanted to jump out of his own body. Giavi cleared his throat. "N-no, boss. Carry on."

"Good."

"I have to ask, boss." Jarrus raised two fingers and leaned forward on the table. "Why are they taking a banking caravan over such a long distance by land? Wouldn't it make more sense to go by airship?"

Crow answered for their employer. "Gor's main bank accounts are on an indefinite hold. Law officials all over the continent are onto his laundering schemes. It's likely why he is opening this account in Cold Brook to begin with."

Jarrus leaned back and crossed his arms. "So, they'll handle his money for a bit of coin off the top."

"Could be," replied Crow. "Or he could have sold them on one of his venture capital startup schemes, a common routine of his. Or so I've read."

Vinai chimed in, leaning back in her chair. "He can't go by private airship. He's stiffed one too many sky pirates. They'd take his vessel before he even reached maximum altitude."

"Yet people still make deals with the old sleaze," Nellik said.

Breylu crossed his arms on the table. All turned to face him. "Regardless of his reasoning, Gor's caravan will be moving across the continent for several days. It will be heavily guarded. But under open sky, Gor's vault of riches will pass across the barren desert and through hundreds of miles of the eastern plains before finding the hands of his *legitimate* cohorts." A pause left the hum of the table's central terminal as the only sound in the room. "I say we hit the caravan and take the coin."

Giavi's fingers tapped the table. 'This is such a bad idea,' he thought.

"We should hit them when they are near the end of their journey." Vinai removed her pipe from her mouth. Smoke seeped through her fangs as she spoke. "They will be weary from their travels and low on resources. The mundanity of the road will have brought them a false sense of security. We can exploit this."

Breylu nodded in agreement. "We should attack before they reach the river. Once they are across that bridge, they'll be in Cold Brook jurisdiction and their lawmen will intervene."

Crow projected a map of the proposed area of attack. Blue holographic lines displayed a wide plain before a river crossing.

"This is going to be an infiltration mission," Breylu said. "We'll sneak into the caravan as part of the protection convoy. We'll split into three teams. First, Jarrus and Lynara will set a diversion."

Lynara's gaunt face lit up. "Does this mean...?"

"Yes, Lynara."

"Combustion. Electrocution. Disintegration." With a toothy smile, she leaned back, hands behind her head and feet on the table. "Another day at the office."

Jarrus raised his tin mug. His breath carried a strong scent of whisky that the coffee failed to mask. "I'll back you up better than you back me up, partner."

"Thank you!" Lynara replied.

As Jarrus let out a chuckle, Breylu continued. "While they are preoccupied trying to figure out what is blasting them, Crow, Nellik and I will move in and steal the armored cart with the safe."

"How will we know which cart is holding the safe?" asked Nellik, raising his clawed finger. "I assume they won't paint it a different color for us."

With a grim chuckle, Breylu said, "I don't imagine it will be too difficult. We will go to whichever cart the mercenaries move to protect."

Nellik's eyes narrowed. "Makes sense. In theory."

"Crow," said Breylu.

"Yes, sir?"

"Can you crack that safe?"

"I can crack anything."

"Good. And can you do a Vandeni accent? Gor doesn't hire many Imperials."

With a satisfied grin, Crow replied, "I can do one better," putting extra emphasis on the last syllable in a perfect Vandeni accent. Her skin changed from its natural shade of grey to a soft blue-grey, and her eyes turned from pale-blue to a deep shade of sapphire. "How do I look?"

Jarrus' jaw dropped. His face flushed red as he cleared his throat.

Nellik snarled. And his tongue flickered. "The same ice still flows in your veins. The same colonial blood."

Crow looked down and bit her curled lip. Giavi reached for her hand, but she pulled it away. He hung his head in shame.

Vinai shot Nellik a scathing glare. He refused to meet his fellow Draekalagon's eyes.

"That's not bad," Breylu said, maintaining his professional tone. "Cover up your neck with a scarf or a collar. Make it look like you could have gills."

"Copy," said Crow.

"Vinai." As Breylu spoke the name, he glanced her way.

"Breylu." She beckoned him with an inviting motion of her scaled blue hand.

"Can you keep us covered from above?"

"So long as there is higher ground."

Breylu pointed to the map. "How about the ridgeline to the west?"

Crow zoomed in on the territory. "It's harsh terrain, but you should have a good view of the caravan."

Vinai took a pull from her pipe. The smoke flooded her golden eyes. "I'll leave before Athenis rises to find an optimal position."

Breylu nodded once. "Scratch any merc that attempts to impede our purpose."

"Understood."

Giavi felt a crushing sense of dread as a terrible question sat on the edge of his tongue. "What about me?" he asked.

Breylu looked to him with a grim chuckle. Piercing green light overflowed from his circular specs. "You're our getaway driver, Giavi."

Giavi swallowed the lump in his throat, which became a crater in his stomach. "Okay," he uttered.

IV

The Arsenal

The armory was her happy place. Not only because of the neat rows of grenades, with their flashing lights of blue, green and red. Not only because of the shining rockets packed together in clear canisters on the shelves. Not only because of the glistening bronze firearms with accessories that she had designed, many of which were illegal throughout the continent.

The armory was Lynara Sikora's happy place because it presented an endless array of possibilities. Flamethrowers that could erupt like a geyser, missiles that could cover a small building in a net of electricity, a grenade that could bring down a green mist of molecular acid. "What to bring?" she whispered.

Nellik stood by the heavy armaments on the opposite side. He opened his scatter cannon's chamber. "Bring whatever you think we'll need."

Lynara gave a single shrug. "Could potentially need them all. Life is full of endless possibilities, Nellik. Must always be prepared. Aways be ready."

Nellik shrugged back. "Then just bring your favorites." He shut an eye and looked at the inside of his charge crystal's chamber through his optical system.

"Why, Nellik." She took a step back and pointed to the shelves of explosives. "Can't do that. That's like picking my favorite child."

Nellik removed the charge crystal from his weapon. "Then bring whichever *child* you think will prove the most"—his eyes crawled to her as his reptilian face stretched with a devious grin—"problematic."

Lynara's face lit up as she turned toward the shelves. "Problematic. Problematic. Problematic." She removed several round objects with purple lights from the shelf. "Voltage grenades. Lots and lots of voltage grenades." She began tossing them into her nearby sack and attaching them to her belt. "High powered. Large blast radius. Little-to-no chance of harming the safe or its contents." She stepped toward Nellik, holding three grenades in each hand. "Very deadly, Nellik. To stand near the epicenter of the blast radius would be the equivalent of getting shot by ten shock-cannons. Set to kill."

"Lynara, stand back."

She stretched her arms toward him. "Lots will die. Many more injured. Death and injury are fairly distracting." Her thin brows tightened in an uneven squint. "Aren't they?"

"Yes, Lynara. But could you please...?"

"Great!" Lynara tossed the grenades into her bag.

"Lynara!" He backed off, shielding his face, as if his arms would somehow protect him from an accidental detonation. "Don't throw those in here, damn it!"

"Why not?" She smacked her lips together three times before raising a finger. "Oh, because they are explosive?"

"Yes!"

"Don't worry, Nellik. They're fully stable. Won't ignite unless I press this button right here." She reached to her belt, her finger hovering over the trigger of one of the voltage grenades.

Nellik winced.

"I made them myself."

Nellik lurched forward and pulled her hand away from the electric explosive. "That's... what worries me."

Lynara eyed Nellik with skeptical dismay. Her brow twitched as she said, "Fair," and walked away.

"What else are you going to bring?" Nellik asked as he replaced his charge crystal and rested his ear to the chamber, listening for the electric current in his heavy weapon.

"Hmm." She sifted through the devices on the shelf. "No napalm. Boss didn't like that last time. Maybe some acid grenades, some frags, some tripwires and... oooohhhh." She held a cylindrical device before her eyes, biting her lip. "Hello, old friend."

"What is that?"

"Nail bomb."

"Seems a little simple for your tastes, Lynara."

She gave a throaty chuckle, tossing the device from one hand to the other. "Nothing simple about shrapnel. Shrapnel causes pain. Pain causes distraction. Have we not been over this?"

Nellik's fiery eyes narrowed on the scraggy woman. "Have an extra one of those for me?"

"Here. Take two." She tossed the weapons to Nellik, who raced to catch them before they fell on the ground. He let out a sigh of relief as he held one in each hand.

'Peculiar,' Lynara thought of the reaction.

Nellik locked a triangular attachment under the barrel of his scatter-cannon.

"How's that launcher holding up?" asked Lynara.

"You did good on this one." His tongue flickered as his claw caressed the accessory. "Good for a nasty shock from a distance. A bit clumsy on the aim, but—"

"Clumsy?!" Lynara cuffed her mouth and gasped.

"Yes." Nellik raised his hands. "But, Lynara, it's okay. It's a grenade launcher. I don't expect—"

"No. No. No. No-no-no-no. No!" She felt a crushing urge to dig through the blimp-shaped objects in the metal tubes at the end of the hall, an urge she was swift to give into. "Clumsy? Clumsy? Unacceptable. You get only the best, Nellik."

"Lynara!" His guttural voice boomed across the armory. "You did good. Get over it. Not everything needs to be—"

"There it is!" Lynara found the canister she was looking for. She held it tight to her chest, rocking it back and forth like a restless infant. She shuffled down the hall toward Nellik, making sure to hide the warning written in red by Breylu Dast. "HIGHLY EXPLOSIVE! DETONATION RESULTS UNPREDICTABLE! FURTHER REFINEMENT REQUIRED! DO NOT USE IN FIELD!"

She opened the canister and handed Nellik one of the small missiles, no longer than his middle finger and no wider than his wrist.

"What is this?" asked the Draekalagon.

Lynara's voice shook as she replied, "Hexahydro-trinitro-triazine. Propelled to combustion by three hundred million volts. Guided by infrared tracking."

Nellik looked down at her with a series of rapid blinks.

Lynara stared back, her head tilting shoulder to shoulder. "It..." She searched for words in the sea of chemical formulas and equations that flowed through her mind. "It blows up. If anyone within the blast radius survives, they'll be electrocuted: a different kind of shock wave. And. And. And... it has heat-seeking ability. Take the shot. It'll find the nearest heat source in your range."

Nellik's thin green lips curled with a devious smile. "This, Lynara," he said with a throaty chuckle, "is why we are friends."

She nodded and dumped more of the rockets into his palm.

A thin sheet of grey clouds swirled across the sky, pierced by the mighty blue rays of Athenis, overlooking the plains of eastern Vanda from its heavenly throne. Small patches of blue, grey and reddish-brown grass lay dispersed throughout the cracked hardpan of the terrain. A faint breeze carried dusty scents of cinnamon from the flowering vines on the cliffside. From the top of the cliff, the Moon Shadow Riders looked down on the caravan as it came into view, moving toward the sparse woods to the north, where there flowed a shallow river.

"There's more of them than I thought there'd be," said Giavi, clearing his throat.

"More targets. More potential distractions," said Lynara eagerly. "Good. Good. Very good."

Jarrus gave her a smirk. "Send 'em to me cooking. I'll put on the final seasoning." He twirled his pistol and tipped his hat.

Lynara smiled back. "A day at the office, Jarrus."

"Quiet." Breylu held out a finger and leaned over his trugan, analyzing the caravan. "We only get one chance to get this right." He cuffed his hand to his ear. "Vinai, are you in position?"

"Yes."

"Good. You're our eyes. Keep 'em peeled."

"Copy."

He looked to Crow, who sat beside him on her bright green trugan. "Got those fake ID signatures for us?"

"Yes, sir."

"Good." Breylu leaned over the cliff, watching the caravan like an eagle preparing for the hunt. "According to our operative on the inside, the safe is in cart four, meaning the fourth cart from the back. But I don't trust her. So, we'll give them a scare, and see which one they run to protect." His glowing eyes narrowed on Lynara. "But don't you dare place an explosive on cart four."

"Cart four shall not be touched by my devices. I won't even look at it. Temptation too great."

Breylu looked again to the summit. "Diversion team one..."

Lynara sat up straight on her trugan, chin raised, knowing that he referred to her and Jarrus.

"You're up."

She nodded. "On it, boss,"

Jarrus gave a lazy two-finger salute. They turned their trugan and made their way down the cliffside. The trail was old and unkempt, but the outlaws were skilled enough riders to traverse it without much difficulty. When they reached the plains below, they brought their reins upon the trugan's necks and took off at full speed toward the caravan. The long line of armored carts were about twenty-five meters away from one another, with a dozen armed guards between each vehicle.

As they approached the formation, several armed trugan riders broke from the formation and rode toward Jarrus and Lynara.

"Don't worry," said Jarrus. "This is all part of the plan."

"Why would I worry?" replied Lynara. "Like you say, it's all part of the plan."

"Exactly why there's no reason to worry."

The opposing riders slowed as they approached.

"So why say it?"

"Halt!" one of them shouted.

"Just let me do the talking," said Jarrus.

"And what if they talk to me, Jarrus? Should I just stare at them blankly and nod?"

"What? No."

"But I thought you were doing the talking."

"I said halt!" said the rider again, his hand resting on his holstered pistol.

"Shut up now." Jarrus flashed a beaming grin as the riders approached. He and Lynara brought their trugan to a slow trot. Their claws crunched the dry grass beneath their feet. "Howdy there, partners." Jarrus gave them a wave, bringing his trugan to a stop. "We just broke off from the caravan to check on some suspicious onlookers from across the field. Turns out it was just a couple of farmers." He leaned forward, waving off his own false suspicion.

"I've never seen you around here before," said the burly, mustached Vandeni man in the middle of the five riders. "You say you're with our caravan?"

"That's right," replied Jarrus with a tip of his hat. "We're on special detail, assigned to protect the... cargo." With a smug chuckle, he added, "If you take my meaning."

"You two have been guarding the carts on the inside?"

Jarrus nodded. "Boss' orders. I don't ask questions. I only guard the stash."

Lynara saw the skeptical expression on the faces of the men and women who had ridden toward them and reached to her belt for one of her voltage grenades.

"Mind if we see some IDs?" asked the burly man.

"Not at all," replied Jarrus. He and Lynara handed them their data systems with the fake ID signatures that Crow had crafted.

The mustached man's eyes crawled between the screens and the faces of the two Shadow Riders. "Says here that you're in Iltha Garvik's squad?" he asked with a sneer.

"That's right," said Jarrus.

"Wouldn't mind if I ran that by her, would you?"

"Not at all," replied Jarrus. "Her transmission ID signature is right in that there data system. Just tap the icon on—"

"Nah," said the man. "I think we should ask her in person."

"Oh, umm—" Jarrus cleared his throat. "I guess I don't have a problem with that. Lead on."

"Why don't you lead the way?" he asked with a smug tilt of his head. "*You're* the one guarding the cart, after all."

"Sure." Jarrus let out a nervous titter. "Follow me then, partners."

"How about you?" The man motioned to Lynara with the data system. "Have any problem with that, Miss... Deveka Yarros?"

Lynara raised her hands and shook her head. "Don't look at me, friends. I let him do all the talking."

Jarrus slumped in his saddle and rolled his eyes. "She's... my sister-in-law," he uttered. "She got hit pretty hard by a lawman shock-cannon blast. Hasn't been the same since."

They all eyed Lynara with an odd mix of sympathy and curiosity. She could tell they wanted her to say something. But she could not say anything. She was not supposed to talk. So Lynara just shrugged and rode toward Jarrus, looking toward the violet sky with an upbeat whistle.

Riding through the caravan, Jarrus darted his forest-green eyes around. Curious onlookers watched him and Lynara as they passed with their escort.

Crow's voice pierced their communication systems with static and shrill feedback. "Garvik is in cart thirteen, near the front."

"Great," whispered Jarrus. "Now we just have to somehow convince her that she knows us."

"She'll know you," said Crow. "Just not for the right reasons."

"Reassuring."

"Just set those diversions and lose those nuisances that you picked up. We'll take care of the rest."

Little did they know, Lynara had already started. From the time they passed the first cart, she had slid magnetic disks down the hill that attached themselves to the underside of the carts or within their tire well. These disks did not look like much. She had designed them to pass off as memory chips or central processing units. Innocent tech. But those disks contained a special concoction of chemicals. And when they mixed, a flash of beautiful colors, a gift to those who gathered in these plains, perhaps their last.

Lynara was careful not to slide a magnetic disk under cart four. 'No, no, no. Not cart four. That would make the boss *very* angry. *Very* upset. He could not lose his precious cart four. Too much platinum in there. Boss loves platinum. Especially when taken in vindication.' She continued whistling her happy tune as she prepared another explosive disk.

As they passed a group of especially curious onlookers between carts six and seven, Jarrus hid his face.

"Got something to hide?" asked their burley escort.

"No, not at all," Jarrus answered. "It's just... it's just—"

"They're with me." From out of the crowd stepped Geldra Marlsson. "They were on a scouting mission, fellas. But they've been with the convoy since the beginning. Nothing to worry about here."

Lynara found herself unable to contain her excitement. "Bounty hunter lady!" she yelled.

Jarrus reached behind and made a fist, signaling that he wished for Lynara to hold her tongue.

"You know these two, Marlsson?" asked the man who had grown suspicious of the pistoleer and the demolitions expert.

"I'm surprised you don't," said Geldra with a dismissive chuckle. "They are two of Gor's most trusted associates."

The old man looked back at Jarrus and Lynara with a blush of red in his cheeks and a clearing of his throat. "Sorry for the inconvenience, friends." He returned their ID signatures to them and rode to the back of the caravan.

Geldra stepped toward them and waited for Gor's riders to be out of earshot. "Why the hell aren't you wearing masks?" she asked with a sharp bitterness in her voice. "You do realize that you are wanted by a rival gang, right? *This* very rival gang."

Jarrus shrugged. "Masks would only raise suspicion. Confidence is the best disguise."

Geldra rubbed the bridge of her nose and shut her eyes. "I would turn the both of you in right now if your boss wouldn't blow a hole in my spine."

Lynara's head bobbed from side to side. "That is a troublesome conundrum. Yes."

The bounty hunter sighed and stepped closer, whispering so the passing caravan could not hear. "Listen, I got some information. Two of the squad leaders hold the key card to cart four. I don't know their names. But I can point them out to you if we see them." She looked to Lynara. "So, let's lift one of those key cards. Then you can set your distraction."

Lynara scratched the back of her head. "About that. The distraction has already been set."

"Wait, what?"

"Yeah. Didn't know you were going to chime in. Had to think fast."

Jarrus' eyes narrowed on his friend. "How did you set the bombs? I was with you the whole time. I didn't see you drop anything."

"Discretion, Jarrus. Discretion is the ultimate key to success in my line of work. Explosions are noticeable. The hand that sets them must not be. Or the explosions themselves will never come to be. It's my artistic—"

"Okay, okay, that's fine," said Geldra with a heavy sigh. "Just wait to set them off until we have the key card."

"That is not an option." Lynara tucked in her lips and squinted an eye. "Those bombs. They're on a timer."

"Wait." Jarrus' eyes widened and his jaw sank. "How long did you set the timer for?"

"Oh not to worry." Lynara looked to her data system. "We still have..." She paused and looked closer. "Actually, we don't have much time at all. Nope, In fact, barely any time." She offered Geldra a hand. She cautiously accepted and climbed atop her trugan. "Follow me, Jarrus."

"Where are we going?" he asked, trailing behind as she took off at full gallop.

"Hey, where are you three going?!" asked one of the guards in the caravan.

"They're getting upset, Lynara!" growled Jarrus.

"Let them. They aren't going to be around much longer." She checked the clock again.

"Stop or we'll shoot."

Lynara grinned as she turned around. "Three. Two. One."

V

DEATH FROM ABOVE

Vinai had to pull her eye away from her scope as several carts erupted in a fountain of blue flame and a mushroom-shaped thicket of electricity flashed in its wake. Men and women around the caravans fell to the ground, engulfed by flames, jolting with electricity or pierced by shrapnel. The bright flash of light still lay imprinted on her retina. She could barely see out of her left eye.

"Vinai, come in," said Breylu via transmission.

"Copy," replied Vinai.

"There are two enemy guards heading toward Lynara and Jarrus' position. Can you see them?"

Vinai moved her rifle to her other hand, her off hand, so that she could look through the scope with her right eye. They approached her allies on the ground with pistols drawn. "I see them."

"Make them disappear."

Vinai fired two shots from her rifle upon the enemies. They collapsed as high-powered voltage circulated their bodies and sent them thrashing to the ground.

"Nice shooting, Vinai!" said Jarrus via com.

Vinai looked again through her scope through the thin haze that covered the prairie below. The enemy troop was in complete disarray. Some pulled their allies from the wreckage while others searched the tall grass and surrounding bushes for the adversaries who ambushed them. Some used magnetic devices to check for roadside bombs. A large host gathered around a cart toward the back of the line.

"Breylu," she said. "It *is* cart four. Look how they are surrounding it. Squads of goons are leaving the carts from the front of the line to make sure they are protecting the fourth from the back."

"We need that key card," Breylu asserted. "Geldra, give us a description of the two higher-ups that have those cards."

"Okay," she said. "One is a young Draelek woman. Rather thin. Light brown skin, blue eyes, average height and wearing a black dress. The other is a heavyset Vandeni man. Middle-aged. Mustache. Tan leather gloves. Red hat with a turquoise gem at the center. Leather pants. Light brown eyes. Wait, maybe they're blue. I'm not..."

Vinai followed a target, switching her scope from her right eye to her left, for the bright flash had faded from her vision. "You said a turquoise gem, correct?"

"Yes."

"I got him." Vinai continued to follow the man with her scope. "He's heading southwest, toward the back of the caravan. And he's not alone." She pressed an icon on her scope, which marked the man with the turquoise gem in red. "Crow, got my mark?"

"Copy," she said.

"Good." Vinai zoomed out to analyze the surrounding fray. "Intercept him before he gets to cart four. If he opens the door and gets in, or worse yet, if they tell it to move before you get to him, we won't be able to accomplish the mission."

"We're moving out," said Breylu.

Jarrus, Geldra and Lynara took cover behind a rock. Five of the opposing scouts noticed them and approached with weapons drawn. Jarrus came out from cover and took down two of them. Vinai's sights found the other three. With a pull of the trigger, she dispatched them one by one.

Her aim returned to the back of the caravan. Breylu, Nellik and Crow rode hard toward the enemy. No one seemed to notice their approach at first. They were too busy checking alongside the road for enemies, tending to their wounded and attempting to douse the surrounding flames. One woman noticed Breylu and his team as they drew near. But Vinai eliminated the woman before she could become a threat.

The surrounding guards looked around, trying to discern where the shot came from. In their distrust, one of them pulled out a shock-cannon and shot one of his allies. Vinai nodded as she beheld the internal disarray among her enemies.

Breylu and his team hopped off their trugan as they came to the back of the caravan. They ducked low and attempted to blend in with the crowd. One man approached and stopped

Breylu. Vinai was sure that he could talk his way out of the situation, but time was of the essence. She shot the man dead.

"Help him!" shouted Breylu. His transmission device was activated, so Vinai could hear him. "Someone shot him. It looked like the cannon fire came from over there!" He pointed toward the prairies to the east, in the opposite direction of Vinai. A small band of guards sprinted after their imaginary enemies.

Vinai turned her attention back to the man with the turquoise gem on his hat. "Breylu," she said. "He's getting close to cart four. That crowd is going to part for him."

"Stall him!" ordered Breylu.

"As you wish." Vinai laid down suppressive fire around the opposing outlaw leader. She made sure none of the lethal electrical blasts struck him; it would be difficult to snatch the key if his subordinates moved his body. She had no qualms, however, about the subordinates themselves. The men and women surrounding him dropped like wasps in a winter storm. In fear, the enemy took cover behind one of the bombed-out carts.

"He's stationary," said Vinai, taking a shot, eliminating another enemy. "He's behind the wreckage of cart six. Sneak around and get the drop on him."

"Copy. I still have him marked," said Crow. "We are on our way."

Vinai continued to lay down suppressive fire and warning shots. "I like you right where you are," she said of the man with the turquoise gem.

With each blast of weaponized lightning, she eliminated another man or woman protecting him. She zoomed her scope back to get a better look at the rest of the caravan. Several of the rival gangsters and mercenaries had broken off from the main group. They were heading in her direction. She crouched low and zoomed in on one of them as he looked to his cohorts and pointed to the top of the cliffside where Vinai took cover.

"Breylu," she said. "They're zeroing in on my position. I'm going to move out and engage from another location."

"Understood," said Breylu. "We're moving through the convoy without any trouble. They're focused on saving themselves. We will need some cover fire once we move to take cart four."

"Copy," she replied. "Vinai out."

Vinai stood up and immediately felt danger. Perhaps the Infinite Serpent had delivered a warning of doom. Perhaps it was her reflex enhancement cybernetics. Perhaps it was simply her instincts. But Vinai dropped to the ground as a spiraling stream of lightning flashed over her head. Three more shots followed, striking the rock behind which she hid.

Dust and smoke wafted through the air. Vinai held her rifle tight to her chest as she got as low as possible.

"Hello up there," a Draekalagon's voice said through her transmission device with a throaty chuckle. "I know you can hear me. Let's have a little chat."

"Breylu," Vinai said over her secure communication line. "I'm pinned down up here. A sniper has a bead on my location."

"Well, take care of it," replied Breylu. "Nellik is about to kill the man with the key card. We're gunna have a target on our backs once he does. We need your eyes on us, Vinai."

"Copy," she replied. "Proceed as planned. I'll get you your covering fire."

Vinai took a deep breath and stretched her fingers across the stock of her tarnished brass rifle, her knuckles cracking as her claws gripped the metal.

"Hello..." the rival sniper spoke again, a mocking tone in his voice. "I'm still down here."

She switched her communicator to a nonsecure channel. "Yes, I know." She took a deep breath as the wind brushed over her snout. She curled her tail as tight as she could so that none of it was beyond the cover of the rock. "To what do I owe the pleasure?"

"It seems we are on opposite sides of this conflict, sister of the Serpent." His guttural hiss slithered through the speaker. Vinai hissed back. "But does this mean we cannot settle our differences like the honorable warriors we are?"

She peeked around the other side of the rock. The squad of approaching enemies had her location, no doubt fed to them by the rival sniper. They began to climb up the cliff. She could see their heat signatures with the infrared setting of her scope. But they were behind the rock wall, out of her range.

"If it is an honorable duel that you seek, let us lay down our rifles and meet in the field with swords drawn. As you were once an ordained member of the Ang Vankila, I trust that you are familiar with the codes of righteous combat?"

"I like my view just fine from here, thank you."

Vinai grinned and replied, "I was never much one for sword-play myself. Too messy." As she spoke, a hand came into view as someone scaled the rock wall to come after her. Vinai shot the enemy's appendage at full power and sent him plummeting to his death.

"Nice shot," said the enemy Draekalagon.

"Thank you."

"How did you know I was Ang Vankila?"

"Your manner of speaking, my lord."

He chuckled. "I suppose we always know our own."

She held her rifle close to her chest and released a deep sigh. "Correct."

"What is your clan?" he asked.

"Oglund."

"Of course," he replied with a raspy laugh. "Vinai of Oglund. I had a suspicion." He let a moment of static linger between the two of them on the transmission before he said, "I am Raagnis of Nyith."

With that final word, Vinai clenched her rifle tight. Hundreds of years of hatred coursed through her veins and made her heart quake with seismic rage. The dishonorable cutthroats, the cheats, the barbarians. Nyith was no clan. They were a blight on Draelekar.

She took a deep breath and shut her eyes, falling into a brief meditation to let her anger go. This man of Nyith had brought none of their clans' histories to their conflict, and she should not fall to such primitive thinking. 'Verse Eighty-Four of the Khlavenmor Rune,' she thought. "'Men shall not be judged on the mark of their kin, not by the sin of the father nor the virtue of the mother, but by the merit of their own doing.'"

"And here we are," Vinai finally uttered. "Two Nuurothar with new clans."

"Wandering warrior I may be," Raagnis said, "this affiliation is no clan of mine. 'Honor among thieves,' is a charming saying. But I've found little truth to it in reality."

"You aren't riding with the right thieves."

As the Draekalagon snipers shared a laugh, Breylu's voice came through Vinai's speaker. "You taken care of that problem yet?" he asked. "We're moving toward cart four."

"Raagnis," Vinai said. "Just because we share a distaste for sword combat does not mean that we are not entitled to an honorable duel."

"I'm listening."

"On a count of three, I will come out with my rifle drawn and you will do the same. Whoever remains standing is the winner."

"I like this."

Vinai paused before adding, "But you must tell me where you are. You know my location. I do not know yours. This gives you an unfair advantage."

"No."

Vinai did not expect him to do so, but she kept a tone of disappointment in her reply. "So much for honor."

"There is a distinct difference between honor and stupidity, Vinai of Oglund."

Vinai nodded to herself. "Fine. I will simply have to hope that you miss. If you do, my rifle will follow your shot and withdraw life from your body. Does this sound fair to you, Raagnis of Nyith?"

"Yes."

"Good." She took a deep breath and strapped her rifle to her back. She had no intention of firing it. At least not yet. "On a count of three."

"Understood."

"One... two..."

On two, Vinai leapt over the rock and down the cliffside, intentionally disturbing the terrain to give herself clouds of dust as cover. Raagnis fired. The shot was close, but he did not hit her. As she rolled down the hill, he fired again, this time singeing the back of her coat. But Vinai saw where the second shock-cannon blast had come from. She hid behind another boulder, this one much smaller. A third shot should have come, but it never did.

As she lay in a prone position, she sent out another transmission. "You almost had me there."

"I must say..." His tone was confident yet strained. "I was expecting some sort of deception. But I didn't expect you to jump over the cliff. Well played."

"Yes," replied Vinai, tightening her squint. "A duel of firearms also features feints."

"Indeed," he replied. "Well, you know my position now," he said with a clearing of his throat. "You have evened the odds."

As he closed his statement with a deep exhalation, Vinai realized why he sounded strange. He was out of breath. He had been running. Who knew how far after he took the second shot? Now she was right back where she started. He knew where she was. But she had no idea where he was.

"Vinai, we need you. Now!" ordered Breylu.

"I suppose you are right," said Vinai, stretching her fingers across her rifle again. "On a count of three?"

"This time I count," replied Raagnis.

"As you wish."

"Three."

Vinai reached for her belt.

"Two."

She unfastened one of Lynara's smoke grenades.

"One."

She pressed the button and threw it on the ground. A cloud of smoke encompassed her. Whether in a panic or in an attempt at a lucky shot, Raagnis fired. Vinai watched the streak of electricity as it pierced the grey smoke. She let the imprint of the bolt sink into her mind and she traced the line of lightning to its point of origin, on the other side of the smoke, across the plains, by the woodland border of the river crossing.

She rolled out from under the cover of the smoke and took aim with her rifle at the exact point she had marked in her mind. If she was off by even a few feet, it would be time enough for Raagnis to alter his aim and shoot her down. But Vinai was not off. Her enemy sat in her crosshairs, under partial cover of a tree. A yellow-skinned Draekalagon in a coat and a traditional lord's hat. A sunken expression of shock sat on his face as he gazed upon the cliffside, almost making eye contact with Vinai.

She fired and the wandering warrior fell to the ground, rifle across his chest. Vinai shut her eyes. "Serpent's blessings, Raagnis of Nyith. May you find yourself in the halls of your ancestors, and may they raise a toast to your valiance and honor." She opened her eyes and returned her aim to the conflict below.

VI

ARMED AND DANGEROUS

Nellik looked on with disgust at the scurrying thugs around cart four. Some huddled around the back door. Some ran away in panic. Some shot those who retreated with incapacitation bolts. "Cowards," Nellik whispered. "They don't even have the courage to kill their own deserters." He placed a hand on Breylu's shoulder as they peeked out from behind a piece of debris. "Let's get in there. If they drive the cart off, we'll never catch it."

Breylu held up his hand. "Not without cover from Vinai."

Crow put a hand on Nellik's shoulder. "She'll take care of that opposing sniper. Don't worry."

Nellik grunted and shook away her touch. "I don't worry."

An enemy mercenary noticed them from around the corner. "What are you three doing there?"

Crow was swift to reply in her perfect Vandeni accent. "There are four wounded over there." She aimed her thumb toward the back of the caravan. "We're hiding from the sniper! Please get help."

The woman nodded and ran to find a medic.

Nellik slid his fangs over his lip and nodded, impressed with the hacker's quick thinking and persuasive nature.

An electric blast rained from the cliffside. Vinai was providing cover fire again.

"Alright," said Breylu. "Let's move."

"Hold on," said Nellik. "I got something that will clear the way for us a bit more." He reached into his coat pocket for the grenade that Lynara had given him in the armory, then tossed it into the crowd. After a few seconds, the grenade exploded and sent nails into the surrounding mercenaries and gangsters.

"Not bad," said Breylu as his enemies fell to the ground with screams of anguish.

Nellik's thin green lips stretched with a serpentine grin. "Compliments to Lynara."

"She's always got something up her sleeve," added Crow.

Nellik rolled his eyes. Why did she always have to talk? Why did she always have to interject with her *oh so proper* Imperial accent? Perhaps another nail bomb would strike her. One less annoyance. But first, she had to open the safe.

"Lynara, Jarrus," Nellik said via transmission. "Meet us at cart four."

"On our way," replied Jarrus.

"Double time. We're about to get a lot of heat."

Nellik, Breylu and Crow shimmied their way through the panicking crowd to the back door of cart four. "Am I clear?" Breylu asked.

Nellik surveyed the crowd. "Clear," he said.

"Clear," Crow repeated.

Nellik rolled his eyes again.

Breylu flashed the key card against the magnetic reader, and the back door opened. Two guards inside the tubular armored vehicle raised their weapons. "Hey, what are you...?"

Breylu shot them dead before they could get in another word, igniting the dim cabin of the armored car in flashes of blue and white.

The shock-cannon fire drew the attention of those guarding cart four. "Hold on!" one of them shouted. "Who do you think you—"

Nellik interrupted the man with a blast from his scatter-cannon, sending him and several of his associates surrounding him to the ground, their bodies overflowing with streams of electricity. Breylu turned around and used the key card to shut the door.

A woman in a ruffled black dress sat in the middle of a row of leather chairs, which lined each side. A sheer veil covered one of her hazy green eyes. She cuffed her hand, interlaced at the fingers, to her mouth. "Please. Please don't hurt me. I'm not involved in—in any of this. I just work for the bank."

"Not to worry," replied Breylu with a tip of his hat as his bright green eyes shifted to yellow. "We have no quarrel with you, ma'am." He unlocked the door to the motorist's section of the cart and shot the men in the front seats dead.

She screamed at the sight. Tears formed in her eyes beneath the fishnet veil.

"I'd be quiet if I were you," Crow said, aiming her pistol upon her. "No sudden movements. No calling for help."

"Get to work on the safe," Nellik said, shooing away her brash tone. "I can handle her."

"Of course," replied Crow with a nod. She leaned on the floor and traced her finger around a creased panel. A screen flashing red and purple lights sat in the top right corner. "This is it."

"Crack it," said Breylu as he pulled the dead driver from the seat and took his place. "We don't have much time."

"Copy."

Crow's visor changed to a purple-and-green tint. She fired up her data system, and her fingers began to type at a lightning speed as rows of code formed on her screen. The monitor on the safe flashed with numbers and letters. She was getting in. Nellik did not want to give her credit, but the little greyskin was getting in.

"Damn it," she uttered. The screen on the safe flashed red before turning off. "They activated the emergency lock."

'Or maybe not,' thought Nellik. He turned to the woman in the ruffled black dress. "Was it you?"

"Me?!" she shouted with a sniffle. "How could it be me? I've had my hands up the entire time. I don't care about the damned safe. Just take it and leave me the hell alone!"

"Can you still get in?" asked Breylu.

"I can." Crow activated the drill setting of her utility tool and popped off the screen. "But I'll have to override the emergency lock manually, then plug my system into the safe analogue to crack the code.

"Get on it," replied Breylu.

A powerful impact shook the cart back and forth. The dim blue lighting of the cabin flickered.

"They're hitting us with heavy artillery!" shouted Nellik.

"We're gunna have to get moving earlier than expected," said Breylu. "These armored carts are strong, but they are not impenetrable." He started the engine and began to drive off. It was not as fast or maneuverable as a trugan cart, but it would protect them for long enough to reach their getaway craft.

Hopefully.

"Vinai," ordered Breylu. "Take out those heavy-cannon shooters."

Two loud blasts echoed outside the cart. "Scratch two," said Vinai over the com system.

The cart shook as Breylu drove it over the bumps of the plains. The civilian woman braced herself against the wall to keep from falling over. "Lynara, Jarrus, you're gunna have to join us on the go."

"Got it," said Jarrus.

They drove on through the plains. Shock-cannon fire pelted the vehicle from all sides as Breylu sped toward the river.

"I have to change positions," said Vinai. "I can't be compromised again."

"Double time," said Breylu. "We need your eyes."

"Hey!" shouted Jarrus. "Not to interrupt the party. But would you mind opening the hell up?!" Several loud knocks at the back door rang off the metal plating of the cart.

Nellik sprang to open the door. As soon as he did, a barrage of shock-cannon fire funneled through the doorway. He took cover. Crow ducked under the chair. The civilian woman covered her face and screamed. Nellik fired several shots, then exited from cover to help Jarrus onto the car after he leapt from his trugan. Then, Lynara leapt aboard with the help of both men. As Lynara made her way on, a rider approached from the side and laid a sticky bomb on the door.

"Get down!" Nellik shouted. But the bomb exploded, launching the front of the armored cart skyward and sending the security door flying off its hinges. Lynara fell to the floor from the impact. Nellik took partial cover and fired upon the pursuing enemies. He struck the man who had placed the sticky bomb and backed the others off several meters.

"Everyone alright?" asked Breylu.

"Fine," said Nellik. "The door, however..." He continued to fire upon the pursuers.

"All good here. No complaints. Perfect as platinum." Lynara felt her forehead and pulled away a fingerful of blood. "Giavi is gunna have some work to do later."

Jarrus noticed the civilian in black on the armored cart. "Good here," he said as he looked her up and down. "*Very* good here." He tilted up his hat with his pistol and sat by her side.

"Jarrus Thane at your service," he said with a crooked smile. "It's a pleasure to make your acquaintance."

She stared at him in silence as he crossed his arms and leaned back.

"I understand that this situation can be... distressing for one not used to such things." He placed a hand on her shoulder. "But not to worry. My team and I... we're professionals. We've been through a whole lot worse and lived to tell the story." He leaned closer to her, a determined look in his eyes. "And my, am I glad I did. Because it has led me to someone as captivating as you."

Nellik groaned and took cover, burying his face in the stock of his weapon. "Jarrus," he hissed. "Do you think we can get a bit of your *professionalism* over here? This job is far from over."

Jarrus tipped his hat. "Of course. Much obliged." He stood and turned to the woman with a slight bow. "You'll have to excuse me for a moment. Duty calls. But please save a seat for me. I'd like to hear more about you."

Jarrus rolled into the doorway and took a crouched position, firing both pistols at their pursuers. He could aim in two directions at once and hit moving targets from twenty meters away. Between Jarrus' pistols, Lynara's grenades and Nellik's scatter-cannon, the Shadow Riders left a wake of death behind them.

"How are we looking back there, Crow?" asked Breylu.

"I'm almost through the emergency lock," she answered. "Just keep them off me a little longer."

"Lynara."

Her eyes fluttered to the Draekalagon man, a grenade pin in her mouth. "Hmm?"

"Can you blow that safe open? It would get us out of here faster than... whatever *she* is doing."

"No!" Crow shouted, her frosty blue eyes glaring upon Nellik. "This safe has a self-destruct component. It will blow if anything pushes out the final lock from the outside."

"So, the platinum will be destroyed?"

"Along with *us*."

"As you were."

Crow returned her attention to the drill.

"Uhm," said Nellik. "Could the shaking of the cart cause you to make a mistake and activate the self-destruct?"

"No, but you distracting me could." She looked back at Nellik with cold resentment. "So shut up."

Nellik nodded and turned his attention back to the oncoming enemies. He reached into his breast pocket for a mine that Lynara had made for him. He threw it out the door and watched for the oncoming attackers to pass its range. When they did, a web of voltage sprang from the ground and sent several thugs toppling off their trugan. Those behind them had to halt and go around the trap. Lynara and Nellik looked to one another, snickering in delight.

Breylu addressed the gang in the back. "Two heavy-weapons men on the west side. Take them out."

Jarrus nodded. "On it." He leaned out of the doorway, keeping his balance with one hand, and fired several shots to the west. He swung back inside, twirling his pistol. "And down they go." He turned to the woman in the dress and sat by her side once more. "Do you know how gorgeous your eyes are?"

"Umm—"

"I find myself lost in them. They shroud you in mystery, yet they are inviting me into your very soul. It's like I have known you forever."

"Ummm—"

He chuckled and leaned close to her. "I think that veil helps with the sense of mystery. It's like you want me to know more. But you'll never just tell me. Is that right?"

She swallowed and shook her head. "I don't... I don't know. It was a gift from my mother."

Jarrus smiled. "Well, your mother is a smart woman. She knew that the angelic traits that she passed to you would be too much for some to bear." He reached for her hand. She gasped but did not pull it away. "But not for me." He leaned closer yet. "No, not for me."

Nellik's tongue flickered as he bared his fangs. "Jarrus."

"Right, be right there." Jarrus leapt back to the doorway and continued to fire upon their pursuers.

Nellik could not help but notice the woman gawking at him as he exhibited his flashy pistol twirls and no-look shots. 'Unbelievable,' thought the Draekalagon.

"They're backing off!" shouted Breylu

"Look there!" Lynara pointed to the line of enemies behind the trugan. "Rocket-propelled weaponry. The cart is degraded from repeated shock-cannon blasts. That artillery will tear right through the armor. And us too."

"Vinai," Nellik said into the com. "Have you reestablished your position? We need some rocketeers taken out."

"Negative," she answered. "There's a squad right on my back. I'm trying to lose them."

"Nellik!" Lynara tugged on his sleeve. "The micro-missile. Use the micro-missile."

Nellik grinned as he switched his scatter-cannon to the grenade launcher setting. "I like the way you think." He took aim and fired. The petite missile spiraled across the plains and struck the ground in front of the opposing artillery. Nothing happened. It was a dud. It must have been a dud.

But then, a mushroom-shaped explosion erupted from the ground, sending their enemies launching into the air. Following the explosion, a net of electricity flung up from the impact point, shocking any the initial blast had neglected. Lynara and Nellik celebrated. But the electricity did not dissipate. A secondary electrical burst surged from the ground, traveling up the waves of mist like a reverse bolt of lightning. Within seconds, the blasts grew powerful enough to reach the armored cart.

"Everyone down!" Nellik shouted.

The vehicle skidded back and forth. The armor of the cart popped, then fizzled. The lights went out. Sparks rained from overhead. Jarrus was quick to wrap his arms around the screaming civilian woman, protecting her from broken glass and any incendiary material. The windows broke on the driver's side of the vehicle. Two of the tires popped. And through it all, Crow's concentration did not break. Her data system was wired into the console on the safe. With one hand, she moved the colored wires from one connection to the next. With the other, she typed on her data system.

"What the hell was that?" asked Breylu.

"A new piece of tech that Lynara developed," answered Nellik. "Very effective. Perhaps... too effective."

"That was the prototype wasn't it, Lynara?" Breylu demanded. "The one that I marked too dangerous for use in the field."

"Indeed," she answered. "As that demonstration just displayed, further refinement is required."

"I'd say so." Breylu turned back around. "But you got them off our backs. So, I'm in no position to complain."

Nellik looked out the door. "For now. Two more squads on truganback are fast approaching. How long until you have that thing opened?"

Several beeps came from the safe as she input codes on her data system. "One minute and seventeen seconds. I have three of five locks broken."

"Make it thirty seconds," said Dast. "We need to unload the platinum."

"Copy that, sir. I'll see if I can expedite the process."

Jarrus held the civilian woman up by the shoulders. "Are you okay? You're not cut or anything?"

She shook her head.

"Good. Don't worry, ma'am. Nothing is going to happen to you on my watch." He leaned back and stretched his arm around her shoulder. "I may live dangerously. But navigating danger is just a day on the job for me."

"It's true," said Lynara, chiming in. "Jarrus can shoot his way out of anything. Quite impressive, really."

Jarrus shrugged. "The girl knows me well."

"If also a little sadistic."

"Lynara!" He shot her a look. She nodded and turned away. "What she means to say is..." He swiveled back to face the woman. "When you're with me, the world is yours. Nothing can slow you down. Nothing is out there to question whether you belong. When you're with me, you have the ultimate gift..."

Her jaw dropped and she backed away as he left his hand outstretched with a dramatic pause. "And what's that?" she finally asked.

"I can't tell you. I'll have to show you." He smiled and relaxed his arm.

"Umm..."

Nellik found himself unable to further contain his rage at this conversation. "Jarrus! Squads closing in. Save this nonsense for when the job is done."

The pistoleer shot to his feet and pulled on his lapels. "Allow me to demonstrate."

Lynara, Jarrus and Nellik fired upon the oncoming trugan riders as they approached. Their enemies' shock-cannon blasts fizzled against the armored truck and through the doorway.

Crow ducked to avoid a stream of incoming fire. "What the hell?! Can you cover me?" she asked, frustration in her voice. "I've almost cracked this. It'd be a shame if I were dead before I could get it open."

Nellik took a weapon in each hand, his scatter-cannon in one and his short-barreled grenade launcher in the other. He fired several shots from the heavy weapons, sending the enemy riders tumbling off their trugan and flying from the explosive blasts. Glee filled his fiery eyes.

"I got it! I got it!" Crow shouted. She flipped open the latch.

Nellik turned around for a glimpse. Mounds of shining metal reflected the dim lighting, as if the vault of the spirit world had opened from the door, welcoming the Shadow Riders into eternal bliss.

"Start unloading!" shouted Breylu. "We're about seventy seconds from the extraction point. From there, we'll have to load and go, or Gor's goons will close in on us."

"Yes, sir," said Crow.

Nellik saw her struggle to lift the minted bars from the floor safe and into the reinforced sacks they had brought aboard the vehicle. He groaned as he went to help the Imperial, loading the heavy bars into the bags so they would be ready to depart at a moment's notice.

The armored cart plowed through the woodland clearing. The river roared below. They were close. And the safe was almost empty. But their enemies were also closing in.

"Everyone hang on tight!" shouted Breylu. Without much time for his warning to settle in, he forced the armored cart into a spinning drift, and left the rear side door facing the river.

Parked along the shoreline was Giavi in a shining chrome speedboat. "What took ye guys so long?" he asked.

Nellik pointed over his shoulder. "Them."

"Oh, gracious me." Giavi ran to the other side of the boat.

"No, Giavi, don't!" shouted Nellik. "We need your help to—"

Before he could finish, Nellik heard a loud barrage of shock-cannon blasts. He peeked out the door and around the corner to find Giavi using the speedboat's rail-cannon to mow down the opposing riders chasing them through the clearing.

"Not bad, kid," said Nellik. "Not bad."

Giavi smiled as he continued to tear through the woodland plains with high-powered streams of electricity.

Breylu came around back, firing his pistol at their enemies. He helped Crow and Nellik unload the platinum while the rest of the gang gave them covering fire. "Is this all of it?" he asked, looking to the bottom of the safe.

"That's all of it, boss," answered Nellik.

"Then let's get out of here."

Jarrus offered the civilian his hand. "May I escort you to our next vessel, ma'am?"

She accepted, her face overcome with both fear and fascination.

"Leave her," Nellik hissed. "She's a liability. She'll slow us down or squeal for help."

"Bring her," Breylu countered. "A hostage could prove *useful*." His eyes narrowed on the woman. "You'll stay quiet, won't you?"

She swallowed and nodded.

The team hopped aboard the skiff. Nellik tossed the last bag on the deck, firing a barrage of shots at the opposing gang as their trugan neared the shoreline.

"Punch it, Giavi!" ordered Breylu.

Giavi fired up the electro-engines, and the boat took off downstream.

VII

The Triggerman

The boat slashed through the whitewater crests on the river. With a rhythmic hiss, the electro-motor left the enemies of the Shadow Riders behind. The slender trees of the woodlands loomed over the river, their grey leaves fluttering in the wind. Amphibious yellow canaries dived in and out of the water with fish in their mouths and chirped from their nests in the trees, sharing the catches with their young.

A refreshing spray of freshwater found the face of Jarrus Thane. "So, there I was," he said, his arm around the back of the civilian woman's chair. "Surrounded by three lawmen in an alleyway. They told me to drop my cannons, that I was under arrest. I told them that I'd rather go down fighting. So, they said if I could draw my cannon before they did and get three shots off before any of them got one, they'd let me go."

"You..." She cleared her throat. "You shot three lawmen?"

Jarrus raised his hands. "On incap of course." He chuckled and looked down.

"I don't believe you." She raised her chin, a sudden aura of confidence in her voice. A confidence that Jarrus found himself drawn to.

"I ain't one for tall tales, ma'am. If I tell a story, that's the way it went down."

She turned away. "I think you are only trying to flatter me... to impress me."

Jarrus smiled and adjusted his lapels. "What's your name, ma'am?"

She glanced back at him. Only for a moment. "Katerin."

"Katerin." With a crooked grin, he declared, "I like that name. Katerin." He leaned closer and lowered his voice, in both pitch and volume. "You see, Katerin. You are not wrong. I am trying to flatter you. And I am trying to impress you. But not with deceit. Only with my humble self, as I live and breathe."

"I'd hardly call you humble."

"I can accept this as a valid criticism."

She faced him again and looked him up and down. "Why do you care so much about impressing me?"

"Well, because I find you impressive."

"How? We only just met."

"I'm not sure yet," Jarrus said with a tilt of his head and tip of his hat. "But I do intend to find out."

Katerin's cheeks flushed purple in a blush. She tried to turn away to hide her face, but it was too late. That is when Jarrus decided to step away. "Always leave them wanting more," he whispered to himself.

"Guardians, damn them all to hell!" screamed Breylu as he tossed the sack against the side of the boat. The platinum slammed against the metal wall with a loud clang.

"What is it, boss?" asked Jarrus.

"It's short," replied Breylu with a distorted sigh. "The safe was short."

"How short?"

Breylu's glowing eyes turned from Jarrus to Crow. "What's the final count of the sacks you were counting?"

Crow separated the shining bricks and coins on the deck, laid out before her crossed legs. "Sixteen thousand seven hundred and eighty-five."

"Nellik, what about you?"

"Twenty-one thousand." Nellik stuffed his last handful of platinum coins into the sack. He lit a cigarillo, then looked to Breylu. "How about in yours, boss?"

"Twenty-eight thousand two hundred and fifteen," he uttered with a growl under his breath.

"Sixty-six thousand," declared Crow. "About a third of what was supposed to be there."

Breylu stared on Katerin, arms crossed. "Where's the rest of it?"

She gasped and looked away.

The leader of the gang sidled toward her, his heavy boots thumping against the deck.

Katerin cleared her throat. "Mister Gor expected that the caravan may attract attention."

Breylu's hand hovered over his holstered pistol.

"He ordered that the platinum be split between three armored carts!"

"And why are you just mentioning this now?" He loomed over her, his glowing green eyes narrowing to thin slits, like the eyes of a snake.

"Umm, I just... I don't—"

"Friends, friends, friends." Jarrus stepped into the middle of the boat, gesturing to his fellow Shadow Riders. "Let us not fret. Sixty-six thousand platinum is no measly sum. That still leaves over nine thousand for each of us before expenses." He cleared his throat and looked at his boss. "I assume that the twenty percent for expenses is still being deducted?"

"You're damn right," said Breylu. "I got a business to run here."

Nellik sighed, gazing upon the river. "At this rate, I'll never be able to pay the boss what I owe."

Jarrus tipped up his hat and made eye contact with the rest of his gang. "This was a successful day, friends. We got a decent chunk of coin, we hit Gor where it hurts, all of us are alive *and* we saved a beautiful woman from danger."

"I was just fine before you came along, thank you," said Katerin.

"Even if..." Jarrus held up a finger. "Some, if not all, of that danger was caused by us."

Breylu sat down and looked to the floor, nodding to himself. "Jarrus is right. It's not the amount we hoped for. But this was a successful venture, and we should treat it as such." His eyes crawled upward and found the rest of the gang. "I think we should also donate five percent to a charity of choice."

Nellik rolled his eyes. "Again?"

"Yes. Again. When we thrive, we share our favor with those less fortunate than us. Riches are a gift. Gold and silver rivers flow. Fortune shared with all."

"Don't you dare quote Draelek poetry at me."

"I just did."

Jarrus put his foot on the gunwale and looked to the horizon. "I shall donate my charity share to the Vulture Shelter for Displaced Parents and Children. As usual."

Lynara glanced up at him, one eye held at a tight squint. "You always give your share to the Vanden Escorts' Guild."

He punched her in the shoulder. "Lynara. Shut up."

"'To keep the girls comfy when you can't be home for them.' Yep. That's what you always say!"

"Lynara!"

His eyes swiveled to Katerin. And Lynara's eyes widened. "I mean, yes. Of course. Women and children." She turned away with an awkward chuckle.

Vinai's voice came through the speaker. "I'm at the rendezvous point. The trugan cart is ready."

"We'll be there shortly," replied Breylu.

"Oh no," said Crow, looking at her data system.

"What is it?" asked Breylu.

"Marlsson. She's been captured." She turned her data system around and pointed to the screen. A red flash on the map marked the location of the tracker that Giavi had inserted under her skin. Crow cuffed her hand to her ear. "She knows we're listening... she's trying to feed us information." She paused before reciting, "Nine mercenaries. Most of them injured. All armed with a wide array of weaponry." She sighed. "They're going to torture her for information."

Nellik shrugged. "She doesn't know anything that can harm us. Why do we care?"

Crow's eyes narrowed on him. "Yes. But they don't know that."

"Not our problem."

Breylu crossed his legs and leaned forward. "I agree with Nellik on this. Marlsson fulfilled her purpose. What happens with her now is out of our hands."

Crow pursed her grey lips. "She held up her end of the bargain. I think we need to hold up ours. We promised to protect her."

Breylu shook his head. "She knew the risks."

"But..."

"Drop it, Crow," said Nellik with a hiss.

Giavi turned around and added in a lighthearted tone of voice, "I think we ought to go back for her. She was instrumental in allowing us to infiltrate the caravan and provided us with crucial information. We owe it to her—"

"No one asked you, Giavi."

"Sorry, Nel." He resumed his position at the wheel.

Lynara leaned back and looked skyward. "Any chance that those nine raggedy gangsters have any more of the platinum?"

"Umm, no," uttered Crow. "Not likely, no."

"Then I vote no." Her gaze returned to Crow. "Wait, if we go back for her, can I utilize explosive tactics to bring about our enemies' demise?"

"I... would imagine that we would not want to risk hurting Geldra Marlsson if we return to aid her."

"Yep. Still a no." She looked skyward again.

"I never put forward a vote on this," said Breylu with a shake of his head. "But we seem to be doing it anyway." He eyed his pistoleer. "Jarrus, please put this to rest."

Jarrus removed his pistols and twirled them, aiming at an imaginary enemy. "I say we go after Geldra Marlsson."

Nellik and Breylu looked to one another in mutual dismay.

"We ride in in a blaze of glory and bring Geldra home." He gave Katerin a smirk and a wink. "If only because it'll make for a good story."

"That leaves us with a tie," said Breylu. He cuffed his ear. "Vinai, what do you—"

"We're going after Marlsson," said Vinai via com system. "I'll prep the trugan."

"Okay," said Breylu with a groan. "So it shall be done."

Jarrus returned to his seat by Katerin's side. "Once we go get our friend, you can go home. It'll be like all of this never happened."

She looked up at him through her veil. "I somehow don't think I can ever forget this."

"Well." Jarrus smiled and shrugged. "Let's hope you only remember the good parts."

"Yes," she said with a subtle simper. "Let us hope."

By a sharp river bend, their enemies had gathered. More had come since Marlsson had fed the gang information via her tracking chip. There were at least fifteen of Gor's gangsters gathered around. They had Geldra in electro-chains, propped against a supply bag. One of the women questioned her. She had bruises on her face and a busted lip.

The Moon Shadow Riders took cover in the bushes by the river, about fifty feet from the campsite. Vinai of Oglund had climbed one of the trees. At Breylu's command, she rained sniper fire upon the campsite, striking dead the mercenaries and gangsters who had gathered around. They attempted to take cover behind their trugan or scurry for the trees. But Vinai had a high vantage point; they could not find cover that was out of her sight. The fear on the faces of their enemies brought Jarrus a grim chuckle.

One of the men ran behind Marlsson and stood her up, holding a shock-cannon to her head. "Everyone stop!" he ordered. "Stop firing or she dies!"

Breylu's calm voice came through the Moon Shadow Riders' communication system. "Vinai, hold your fire."

She did as instructed.

The burly man holding Marlsson hostage was the same who had escorted Lynara and Jarrus through the caravan when they had first arrived. "Fire another shot and she dies!"

"I have a clear shot, Mister Dast," said Vinai via the communication system. "Give the word and I'll put an incap bolt in him. Worst-case scenario is that Marlsson gets knocked out too."

"Only if he makes a sudden move," said Breylu.

"Copy."

"We don't need to settle this like savages," said the burly man. "We can settle this like honorable ladies and gentlemen." A grin found Jarrus' face. "A duel," he said. "Our best versus your best."

"I think we can arrange that," declared Breylu. He turned to his top cannon. "Jarrus. You voted to bring us out here. Care to flash some of those pistol skills?"

"It'd be an honor." He stood up and adjusted his bow tie before beating the dust from the shoulders of his coat. He looked to Katerin. "Now you will find that no tale is too tall when it comes to my line of work."

His boots crunched the grass and dead leaves. When he reached level ground, his stride turned to a dignified sashay. One of the five surviving enemy outlaws stepped toward him. She pulled back her grey duster to reveal the brown handle of a pistol. Jarrus recognized the attachment on top of the weapon; it was a laser sight. 'Gotta make sure we can keep this in close range,' he thought.

"I have a few stipulations." Jarrus stepped back and forth, raising a finger. "One, I don't want you with that weapon against our lady's neck during the course of this duel." He held up another finger. "And two, I want to set the range of the duel at ten meters."

"What's in it for us?" asked the opposing duelist.

Jarrus flashed them a beaming grin. "Well, all five of you can compete against me at once."

"What?" said Nellik via com system. "Jarrus, what are you doing?"

"You're a brave man," said the burly man. "But just how brave? What do you say we run this duel riverboat rules?"

Jarrus shrugged. "I would have suggested town hall rules myself. But I suppose the undertaker in Cold Brook could use a bit of extra work."

Geldra Marlsson's eyes widened on Jarrus. "Are you insane?" she mouthed.

Jarrus flashed her a wink.

"Jarrus," said Vinai via com. "The big one no longer has his pistol on Marlsson. Want me to take them out?"

"No," whispered Jarrus. "I got this."

"He made his bed," said Breylu. "Let him sleep in it."

The opposing gang members laughed and formed a line around the woman in the grey duster. "Five against one," she said. "You truly are as foolish as they say."

"And yet I am still here standing."

"For now."

"Yeah," he said with a wry smile. "For now."

The burly man unfastened his pistol. His fingers twitched over the handle. "Any last words?"

"If these words are to be my last," uttered Jarrus, hiding his eyes beneath the brim of his hat. "May they last a lifetime."

"Whatever that means." He scoffed and turned sideways. "Draw on three, boy."

Jarrus checked his pistols' lethality toggles to make sure they were set to kill, as the rules of the game dictated.

"Three."

He looked back at Katerin, who watched with a sunken jaw, her eyes clouded with concern. He gave her an assured nod.

"Two."

Jarrus' hands twitched over his pistols. He inhaled.

"One."

And he exhaled.

"Draw!"

Jarrus rolled forward in a summersault. In one motion, he came to a kneeling position and drew his pistols. In a series of consecutive shots, he discharged his weapon upon his five opponents. The blasts roared across the plains, followed by echoes of thunder. The enemy men and women were on the ground, writhing in electric pain before they had managed to raise their weapons. Two of them had yet to even draw their pistols.

"Nice work, Jar!" declared Lynara, who leapt up from the cover of the bushes to stand at his side.

Jarrus tossed his pistols in the air before giving them a twirl and reholstering them. "Y'know, no one ever declares that you're not allowed to take evasive action at the start of a duel. Yet I do it every time, and then they have this look of shock on their face."

"And in their face. And across their entire body."

Jarrus and Lynara shared a laugh before he turned his attention to Katerin. She looked at him, covering her mouth.

He approached with caution and offered her a tip of the hat. "Are you okay?" he asked.

"Yeah, it's just..." She stuttered and fanned herself. "I've never seen anyone shoot like that before."

"Few have," said Jarrus with a tilt of his head. "You didn't know them, did you?"

"I did," she answered. "But we weren't close... or anything."

"Excuse me?!" Geldra Marlsson shouted. "Will someone get me out of these damned chains?"

Breylu took down his mask to light a cigarillo. "Crow, get on that," he ordered.

"Yes, sir."

Breylu looked at Nellik and Giavi. "Search their bodies. Take anything useful. Then let's get out of here before the cavalry arrives. We made enough noise to attract lawmen from three jurisdictions."

After Crow freed her from her chains, Geldra wrung out her wrists and approached Breylu. "Thanks for coming back for me. I really do appreciate it."

"Don't thank me," he said. "Thank Crow, Giavi, Vinai and Jarrus."

Geldra turned to Crow. "Really? You?"

Crow nodded.

"Go figure."

"They don't have much," shouted Giavi. "A couple coins and some weapons."

"Take their data systems," said Crow. "I can hack into them and figure out Gor's next move."

Breylu turned to Geldra. He removed his specs, though his eyes still glowed green. "Any chance you can give the civilian a ride? The gang and I won't be coming through Cold Brook for quite some time."

"I can do that," she said, turning to Katerin. "I'll drop you off just outside the city. Gor's men will be looking for me now as well."

Katerin nodded.

"Come on," shouted Breylu. "We're moving out." He glanced back at Geldra once more. "Once you're done, await a signal from Crow. Follow it and meet us for further briefing."

"Understood," replied Geldra.

Jarrus stepped before Katerin, hand on his waist. "Sharing this journey with you here today has been of the utmost privilege to me. I hope that I have given you stories to share with your folks and your friends for years to come."

Her eyes widened and she flashed him a nod.

"But if you ever decide that a taste just wasn't enough, and that you would like to see more, feel free to reach out through the satellite network." He reached for her hand and bowed. She tensed but did not pull away. "Just say the word. I will show you a side of life beyond your wildest dreams." He leaned over and gave her a soft kiss on the hand. Her skin fell to a chill as she let out a gasp. "Farewell."

"Jarrus!" shouted Nellik. "Let's go!"

Jarrus released her hand and tipped his hat. He watched Katerin walk away with Geldra before he turned around. With a deep sigh, he walked toward the trugan cart, where the other Shadow Riders and the platinum they had earned for the day awaited.

"Gor is quite angry," said Breylu, sitting at his desk with his hands crossed. "He's offering fifty thousand platinum for my head. More than double the legal bounty."

The Shadow Riders laughed with their leader, except Giavi, whose troubled blue face fell to the floor.

"How do you feel, Miss Marlsson?" asked Breylu.

"Much better." Geldra rubbed the back of her neck. "Thank you for taking that thing out of me." She gave Crow and Giavi a thin smile.

"I do apologize for having to resort to that in the first place," said Breylu with a bow of his head. "But you proved yourself useful and honest. So we took it out as a sign of good faith."

"Thank you."

"Along with this." Breylu passed her a satchel filled with coins. "Consider it a payment for your efforts thus far and a retainer of your services."

Crow approached Geldra and attached a small grated device to her lapel.

"What's this?" she asked.

"A new tracking-and-listening device," said Crow. "Boss said we needed to keep *just* a bit of insurance."

Geldra crossed her arms. "What happened to good faith?"

Breylu's eyes narrowed. "Would you prefer it back in your neck?"

She sighed. "I suppose not."

"I didn't think so." He waved her off. "Go to Vulture and await further instruction. I want you to listen for any word on Gor's weapons caches and bank transfers."

"It's not like I have an in with Gor anymore, Dast."

"Just keep your ears open," said Breylu. "People are loose lipped in a saloon. Hang around the watering holes. Report to me on what you hear."

"You got it." She stepped toward the door and turned around. "Thank you all," she said. "Thank you for coming back for me."

"The Shadow Riders take care of their own," said Vinai, leaning against the wall.

"Thank you for your *continued* loyalty," said Breylu.

Now surrounded by only his gang, Breylu leaned back. "Take a few days off. We'll reconvene here at the stronghold for another meeting once the dust has settled a bit." He held up a finger. "If you go into any towns, keep a low profile. Things are pretty hot for us after that job."

"Well worth it," said Nellik. "I think I'll buy myself a new saddle. A leathersmith in Ash Valley embosses his designs with electrum plating. They are quite nice."

"With what coin?" asked Breylu, displeasure in his voice. "You still owe me money, even after I take your share from the Cold Brook job."

"Well, I thought I'd pay you in part..." Nellik's eyes narrowed and his snout flared. "And keep a bit for myself as a reward for my efforts."

"Go ahead," uttered Breylu. "And I'll start charging you interest on your debts."

Nellik groaned and fell back into the soft blue cushion of his chair.

"Good work, everyone," said Breylu. "Enjoy the time off. You've earned it."

Everyone began to step out of the room.

"Anyone fancy a game of depth strike?" asked Giavi.

Lynara waved him off. "No can do. Very busy. Must refine the micro-missile. Death to others. Not to us. Key to great success."

"I'll play a round with you, Giavi," said Crow.

"Jarrus, stay here for a moment," said Breylu.

Jarrus held his place in the doorway before stopping and turning around. "What can I do for ya, boss?" The door shut behind him, leaving the two men alone.

"You voted to go back for Marlsson. Why?" Breylu leaned forward on his desk, his specs catching the blue light of his data system. "That's not like you."

Jarrus gave a dry chuckle and a shrug. "Like you always say about loyalty, boss—it's what holds this gang together. Marlsson showed loyalty to us, even if it was... under duress."

"It had nothing to do with that banking woman, then?"

"What? Pff." Jarrus placed his hands on his waist and looked down. "Not a chance, boss. Not a chance."

"Understood." Breylu leaned back. "What are you doing for your time off?"

"I'm gunna ride up north and spend a few days in Meadow Springs. Beautiful up there during the summer seasons."

"Very good."

Jarrus caught a glimpse of the screen on Breylu's desk, displaying his digital file on Kasta Krane.

"I'll see you in a few days, Jarrus," said Breylu. "Enjoy your trip."

Jarrus nodded and turned around. He paused at the automatic door before glancing back at Breylu once more. He found himself unable to stop himself from speaking. "Hey, boss, why don't you come with me?"

Breylu looked up. His green eyes brightened in shock. "I'm sorry?"

"Come with me. You could use some time off as well. Enjoy yourself for a few days, then we'll get back to work."

Breylu let out a staticky sigh and gave Jarrus an enigmatic glare. Then he shook his head and looked down at the screen. "Too much to do, Jarrus. I have a business to run here."

Jarrus nodded. "Send me a transmission if you change your mind."

Breylu did not respond. His eyes shifted to the screen, to that file, that file that he had spent hours, years rummaging through, adding to, obsessing over.

As the door opened and Jarrus turned the corner, he heard Breylu utter, "'Paved with shadow, paved with ashes, paved with brimstone, the black road is all I know.'"

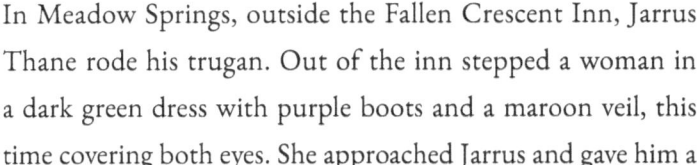

In Meadow Springs, outside the Fallen Crescent Inn, Jarrus Thane rode his trugan. Out of the inn stepped a woman in a dark green dress with purple boots and a maroon veil, this time covering both eyes. She approached Jarrus and gave him a hesitant nod.

"Katerin," he said with a tip of his hat and a welcoming grin. "What a pleasure it is to see you again."

"Likewise," she replied with a bite of her lip, nervous apprehension in her voice. "So, where are you taking me?"

He leaned forward on his trugan and offered her a hand. "Everywhere. Anywhere."

After hesitating for a moment, she accepted his hand and climbed onto the back of his saddle. "What does that mean?"

Jarrus turned around and flashed a devious grin. "Whatever we want it to mean, darling." He traced his hand across the radiant stars of the amethyst-and-sapphire night sky. "That is the definition... of freedom..."

Author's Note

What a ride! This story was absolutely thrilling to write, as I did a lot of things that I normally would not do. I switched perspectives (and every chapter at that). I wrote in short form without any goals of putting this work in a collection. And I set out to write a novella that actually ended at novella length. Typically, my short stories become novellas, my novellas become novels and my novels become epics that I need to purchase more cloud space for.

If you had met the Shadow Riders before, I hope you have a new appreciation for who they are as individuals and to one another. If this was your first run-in with the outlaws, and want to see more of their devilish mischief, check out *Folktales from the Endless Frontier Volume 1* and *Endless Frontier: The Hunter and the Knight*. Follow Nellik as he seeks a dueling partner to help punish some card cheats and see if Breylu manages to track his prey: the elusive Kasta Krane.

If you have not done so already, please sign up for my mailing list at brettlurie.com to receive news on events and signings, writing progress updates and free stuff!

Please leave *The Cold Brook Job* an honest written review. I cannot express enough how important it is for an author to get reviews from readers like yourself. Not only is your feedback immensely valuable, but reviews bring my books to new eyes. If you have enjoyed your time in Vanda, there is much more to come!

If you would like to chat about my writing, share your reactions to the stories, theorize about the paths of the characters or even just say hi, feel free to contact me at:

brettlurie@brettlurie.com, or find me on Facebook, Instagram or TikTok.

Until then, farewell.

About the Author

B rett grew up splitting his adventure appetite between fantasy quests through Tolkien's vistas and Eastwood standoffs in Sergio Leone westerns. His debut weird western saga, *Endless Frontier* pulses with reverence for flawed protagonists, supernatural showdowns, and mystical science magic. A scholar of political theory during his academic studies, Brett chose to apply his knowledge of statecraft to his woldbuilding.

An avid RPG gamer and comic book collector, Brett brings captivating women leads, amphibious races, and a magic system based on wireless electricity powered by charge crystals. With an endless frontier to explore, Brett looks to expand tales of high-voltage rivalry and unlikely alliances. His happy place is in the mountains with a cup of coffee on the table and his cat, Raven, on his lap.

www.ingramcontent.com/pod-product-compliance
Lightning Source LLC
Chambersburg PA
CBHW021929170626
46807CB00007B/3034